CASSIE LEIGH

Business Casual

AN INK & BRAZEN WOMEN NOVELLA

Sassy Typewriter Press
5001 1st Ave SE
Ste. 105 #243
Cedar Rapids, IA 52402
https://sassy.typewriter.press/

ISBN 978-1-940509-28-0

Version 2.0.0

Briar Goodall learned to be perfect. She lost her identity becoming the kind of wife and daughter anyone would desire, but they left her anyway and took everything on the way out. Starting over in a new city with a new job, she trys to fit in and be invisible. To her new boss, real estate heir, Ciaran Rand she stands out for all the wrong reasons. With him she wants to get under his skin and to rub herself all over it. They're in a war over the dress code policy that has her breaking a few rules as she travels the path to self-discovery, seeking a love that can handle her both in and out of business casual.

Authors Note

This novella was originally released in February 2018 in a limited run with the Seduction In A Suit Anthology which is now out of print. I have edited it further and added a brand new epilogue that was not part of the original release and exclusive to this edition. I feel like this version is much improved even though the changes ultimately are minor. Sometimes the smallest things make the biggest impact. Thank you for choosing my book.

Chapter 1

STEP ONE OF MOVING ON WHEN LIFE FALLS APART IS to turn to loved ones for support. At least that's what Briar Goodall would have done if her family hadn't been the reason her life had fallen apart. So instead, step one was starting over around friends.

The door swung open to a friendly smile that made her heart want to burst with relief. Briar waved the drink caddy under Gigi's nose in offering. "Pumpkin Spice Latte season is better than sex. It's the least I could do to thank you."

Gigi stepped aside allowing Briar to shimmy past. Thankfully, the kitchen was nearby. The bags she hooked dug into the flesh of her fingers. She dropped the bags and lowered the tray of drinks onto the kitchen counter. She stood massaging the blood back into her abused fingers as Gigi swept into the tiny space.

Briar caught the concerned look that flitted across the typically difficult to read face of the raven-haired temptress that had been a fixture in her life since college—darkness to Briar's own warm sunshine, and perfect. Everything Briar wanted to be. Not because her friend was beautiful, but because she was secure in herself—knew her own mind. Gigi caught Briar watching and the look was gone, locked away behind the neutral smile she wore when she hid her thoughts.

Pulling her drink from the caddy, Gigi inhaled the steam wafting up through the tiny opening in the cup. "Mhmm— thanks for this, but I have to say you're having sex with the wrong people if that's how you feel."

"Please. You met my husband. Mom can have his sorry ass."

Gigi held her cup out and nodded as if to say touché. "Ex-husband, honey. Get used to saying it."

To curb that line of conversation, Briar freed her own cup and turned to survey the room beyond the kitchen. Artwork covered the walls, creating trails of color, like vivid flowers scaling the white placid surface. It should have been distracting, especially with the variety of themes failing to form anything cohesive. Instead, she found it calming. Each new work became a different oasis to escape and lord knew she needed an escape. The art also succeeded—at least for a moment—in distracting the eye from the green velvet sofa and hot pink club chairs that dominated the room. Like the woman it belonged to, the room screamed bold.

Could she borrow that for herself, like she had borrowed this apartment? Fuck—she hoped so because she couldn't continue the way she'd been. "I still can't wrap my head around you letting me stay here. This place is gorgeous."

Not to mention, fully furnished. An important bonus since Briar had driven here with nothing but her clothes, books, and a box of the few memories she hadn't burned before liquidating everything else. Frankly, she would rather not live with the reminders after the way her marriage ended. It made a great bonfire, but now she was ready for the fresh start she'd driven six hours to get.

Gigi twirled the keys on one manicured finger. "It's the least I can do. Besides, I'm staying at Roman's place. I would have been breaking the lease."

"You're welcome, I guess." The keys slipped from her friend's finger and Briar caught them before they hit the counter. "Don't take this the wrong way, but you having a fiancé is still tripping me out. I mean—wow."

Gigi's smile softened, her eyes going round and dreamy. Had Todd ever made her swoon like that? No, but then no one ever did that for Briar. She had yet to feel the kind of joy that appeared to radiate from Gigi.

"Yeah, well it trips me out too, but he's not like anyone else. He gets me."

Hard to be bitter when you hear something like that. It helps to know who you are, something that felt insurmountable to Briar after years of fitting herself into other people's unattainable molds. She swiped at the tears that threatened the corners of her eyes with the back of her hand and took a sip of the creamy spice goodness of her coffee.

"How are you holding up?" There was that concern again, laced through Gigi's tone.

It's what brought Briar here. She had a lot to thank her former college roommate for. When Gigi called to ask her to be a bridesmaid—she'd been thrilled for her friend of course and honored to be asked—but in that first moment, Briar did the unthinkable and burst into tears. Finding your husband cheated and left after clearing out your bank account will do that to a girl.

When she answered Gigi's call, Briar had already eaten half a pint of Java Chip ice cream with more waiting in the freezer. Gigi didn't take offense to the emotional outburst. Instead, several cosmopolitans shared over Skype later, Briar had a place to stay and a job interview courtesy of a favor from the maid of honor. It was the first right step she'd taken.

As it turned out, the money could be recovered—sort of. After her very cathartic bonfire, Craigslist and eBay had served her well for selling off the possessions Todd left behind, along with anything that reminded her of her marriage. In other words everything. And she closed on the sale of her house Friday. Financially, she would recover from this mess. Personally, that was another matter entirely, but Gigi and her new friend, Ann, had her covered there too. So yeah, she could answer her friend with what she wanted to hear without it being total shit.

"I'm doing fine right now. You really don't need to worry." Briar plastered on a smile and turned her back. "Besides, once the private detective finds my ex, I can finally finish the divorce. The whole thing is nearly behind me."

Switching to busy mode, she put down her coffee to start unloading the new kitchen and grocery items from the bags she brought with her. Gigi leaned against the counter, one arm across her breast, hip cocked and eyebrows lifted as if they could say bullshit for her.

Briar peered sideways at Gigi. "What?"

"Do you actually expect me to believe that?"

"I'm fine, really, Gigi. I know I was a mess at first, but even I have to admit my marriage was dead for a long time."

"Honey, your marriage was dead before it started. I told you something was wrong with that guy right out of the gate."

Briar shrugged. Gigi did warn her at the party where she met her ex and every time Todd picked her up after. Briar never took her seriously because Gigi didn't trust any man. Instead of crying wolf it was the party girl who cried cheater. This one time she happened to call it right. The burn still itched like a newly formed scab over an open wound—so easy to scratch loose to bleed again. She imagined that was just how divorce felt. Hers shouldn't be an exception even if the details were the stuff of tabloids.

"So then let's go out. After the guys get here and haul up your boxes, you can hit our spot with us. It's laid back, walking distance, and the drinks are cheap because we know the owner."

"Sounds nice but I'm going to need a rain check. Wouldn't look good to be hung over on my first day at the new job."

"Ah—you'll be fine. Maybe the guys even have a friend. Declan is not attached but I have it on good authority there's history with him and Ann, otherwise I'd set the two of you up."

"No way am I dating my tattoo artist. I'm glad it worked

out for you but that doesn't mean I need a replacement. I'm okay with being alone. No offense."

"None taken—besides I'm not saying you should get back in a relationship, just get back in the saddle. When's the last time you enjoyed a good round of reverse cowgirl?"

Wrong moment to sip her latte—because she had just spewed it on the kitchen island in a burst of laughter. "How the hell do you do that?"

"Oh wow—I'm so glad you're getting divorced if you have to ask me that question."

"No. No. No," Briar stammered through her nervous laughter. "I've done that—that wasn't what I meant." Of course it had been before Todd, who had no imagination past missionary where their marriage bed was concerned. However, he did allow her mother to do that, which scarred her for life for having walked in on it.

A knock on the front door broke the awkward moment. Gigi wagged her eyebrows in a suggestive dance and then glided back to the front door. This time when she opened it, she didn't flatten herself. Instead, she stood half blocking it, so when Roman came through, he had no choice but to rub up against her. He snaked his arm around her waist and pulled her with him as he strode into the kitchen, leaving the door to swing closed. At least it would have if a second tattooed Adonis hadn't hip-checked it on his way in and then mule kicked it closed behind him—the aforementioned friend, Declan.

Briar was familiar with both men. Each time she made the road trip for the next job interview, she also made a stop to spend a little time under Declan's tattoo machine. These men were different in every way from the slick frat boys and the corporate set that she and Gigi associated with back in the day. They were the new breed of modern hipster—Roman, with his plain white t-shirts and cuffed jeans, working alongside Declan, his best friend and business partner sporting his on-trend beard, fedora and dark sunglasses. They were serious artists, who turned their passion into a thriving business in an up-and-coming neighborhood, one she was now a part. It had changed Gigi for the better. Briar couldn't help but hope it might do her the same good in its own way.

Roman clapped his hands together. "I hear there's a truck to unload. Where is it? I didn't see a U-Haul."

"I don't actually have a whole lot." Briar's cheeks flushed with her embarrassment. "I sold or burned most of our stuff. I just have some tote boxes in my car. I told Gigi not to call you. I could have handled it."

Great guy that he is, Roman held out his hand with a grin. "Don't sweat it. Hand over the keys and we'll take care of it. You just buy us a drink after. Fair?"

She just told Gigi no, but how could she say no to that deal? Guys like this gave her hope. Todd would have left and been pissed at his wasted time. She'd been so busy trying to be perfect that she'd overlooked his shallowness. It was only now, held up in comparison with such a stark contrast, that she could see it. The friend who wanted nothing to do with love had chosen better for herself than Briar, the girl who would once have given anything for someone to notice and love her.

Briar dangled keys over his waiting hand. "Settle for pizza and beer?"

Roman smiled and took the keys. "Come on, Declan. Let's get this knocked out. I'm feeling the need for some Chicago style."

Yep, this is what she had been missing—friends. For once she might really be fine, even as imperfect as she stood.

Thwap, thwap, thwap. The bowl of the spoon tapped against hardwood and linen. "Are you listening to me, CJ?" The grizzled voice of his grandfather brought Ciaran back into focus.

Instead of the sleek offices of downtown, Ciaran sat in the dining room of his grandfather's turn of the century mansion. People forgot these stately mansions exist in their city, a byproduct of the industrialization his family capitalized on. People remembered Brucemore, a tourist site now. Blocks away, a stone's throw from the American foursquare homes popularized by Sears and Roebuck—another smart investment their family once profited from—these mansions full of the best architecture of the era thrived. The dark stained wood panel wainscoting and navy wallpaper in the dining room they now sat in probably hadn't changed since the place was built. Insulated behind heavy velvet drapes, time seemed to stand still in this room, right along with his grandfather's archaic values.

"Yes, the employee handbook. Update it. Team building event between departments. Got it. I will see that those items are addressed."

Per usual, Ciaran had only listened enough to answer when addressed. His mind was too full of properties and deals. Especially with his father and brother dangling one hell of a property development deal right under his nose. It was the kind of project he'd always hoped they could do together under the Rand Enterprises banner.

"I don't appreciate your tone young man. If you expect to run this company one day I suggest you make an adjustment."

Had they been discussing something a CFO should be concerned about rather than something more fitting of his new HR director—who, by the way, his assistant had scheduled to start tomorrow—perhaps Ciaran could have reigned in his tone and frankly, his attention may not have gone astray. Of course, that would require Jamison Rand Senior to acknowledge that Ciaran had attained a master's degree in business finance and an MBA in marketing or that he was twenty-eight, not eighteen.

"My apologies. I was considering the opportunity this gives me to get to know my new HR director." He kept his smile neutral, or at least he thought so. The scowl growing on his grandfather's withered face pointed to failure.

"The policies that govern your employees are your concern. Don't pass the buck." The old man coughed, a brittle sounding hack, and then pushed away his untouched meal.

Leaning towards his grandfather, Ciaran scrutinized the octogenarian more thoroughly. The CEO of Rand Enterprises might seem invincible to those watching from a casual distance but to Ciaran, who'd grown up at the man's knee being groomed for a legacy that never should have been his, he could see the toll it took on his health. His skin had taken on a waxy sheen and a gray tinge. Hell—it hung from the man's frame, making Ciaran wonder for the first time just how much weight the once robust man lost. He wanted the family patriarch to retire in good health, to live long enough to make him proud and more than that, Ciaran wanted to reunite the broken bonds of his family. Business was his best means—possibly his only means—of bringing his disinherited father and brother back into the fold.

"You're right—I'll see to it." Ciaran answered directly so that he could steer the conversation toward his concerns. "Have you seen your doctor recently, grandfather?"

He beat the bowl of the spoon on the table once, like a judge declaring some kind of verdict. "You won't get this company by declaring me incompetent, young man."

"Not everything is about business. Is it too much to believe I care because we're family?" Ciaran pushed away from the table and stood, hands braced in front of him, palms flat on the smooth walnut finish. "Do you really think I want to lose you too? I had no idea that I came off so damn cold."

Jamison stared up at him unblinking and firm. If he had a shred of regret for his accusation, his poker face held firm. The man was a shark wearing the skin of a modern day robber baron—progress be damned. "Regardless of your feelings my health is none of your concern." The crisp staccato of each word clearly brooked no argument. "But I will remind you of other concerns: your position as CFO of this company, your current assignment, and your dinner with Monica Fitch, the advertising manager of Fitch and Klaussner. As I understand, she stands to inherit quite a sum herself. Think of what a merger through family connection could do for the company, CJ. "

"I really wish you wouldn't call me that. I'm not a ten-year-old boy." Irritation made his polite words clipped as if he bit off each one as it came out.

"Your name isn't proper." Ciaran opened his mouth to speak but the old man was on a roll now. "That Irish woman your father insisted on marrying had to be different. Had to show you belonged to her."

"My mother's name was Maureen."

"Irrelevant—she was too proud to let you be Jamison Rand III. Son, promise you'll leave those Irish ones alone. If this Fitch girl doesn't work out, get yourself a stalwart English girl or German. The German girls are good stock."

"Who I date is not your prerogative, Grandfather." Ciaran balled his fists up. It was all he could do not to say how he really felt—he'd avoid marriage or anything more than casual until he was free to marry the way he wanted—until he earned the keys to the kingdom.

To be clear, Ciaran agreed with the actions his father took. Ciaran may not be able to make the same choice and walk away himself, but he respected his father all the more for having done it, for having made his own way in the world without the money and influence from the Rand family fortune. Jamison Rand Junior started a company from nothing with a young wife and child. He succeeded alone. As far as Ciaran was concerned, it was his father who proved his rightful place as CFO and future CEO—not Ciaran. He lived in that shadow every day and kept his silence.

"Yes—well. I can't wait forever." The hall clock struck the hour. "That's enough for one day. I've had your assistant put the dinner meeting on your schedule. He'll brief you of the details."

Yes—and his assistant already cancelled those plans at Ciaran's standing orders. A fact he was sure to hear about later.

The chair feet dragged across the floor, a deeper version of nails on a chalkboard. Just like that, the matter closed.

Jamison stood tossing his napkin on his plate while Ciaran himself stood fixed in the same position staring at the now empty seat. He blinked and rolled his shoulders back as he straightened. This was not the old man's first casual reminder that he expected Ciaran to marry advantageously—something Ciaran's father failed to do when he married Ciaran's mother heavily pregnant with another man's child—his brother Hamish.

For all his grandfather's fine family ideals, he didn't have an ounce of familial feeling. This was not poison teaching from his mother, as Jamison would have people believe. His mother—God rest her—had never uttered a cross word regarding her father-in-law, no matter what he might be persuaded. Ciaran didn't need her to tell him what he could see for himself. It made him glad that his father insisted Ciaran keep the possible purchase of the vacant factory and their plans for renovation to themselves. The senior member of their splintered clan would have been in no mood to hear it, just as Ciaran's mood to deal with it had soured.

Another lonely weekend wasted and ruined by work. All he could do was hope for a better Monday.

Chapter 2

PARKING IN A NEW CITY IS NOT A VALID EXCUSE FOR being late. After widening her circle for the fifth time, Briar finally found a parking ramp with an opening, but so far away from her destination, she might as well have walked to work. She focused on the metronome click of her heels on pavement matching it to her breathing as she hurried down the sidewalk. Heels—another thing slowing her down. In another life, she had comfortable track shoes and allowed her feet to do the rest. If she could do that now, she didn't need tennis shoes. She'd make it.

"Fuck it. They'll never know."

Briar stopped moving. Reaching out, she braced the tips of her fingers on the brick exterior of the random building she'd been hurrying past and kicked off the black slingback torture devices. She scooped them up, cradling them between her leather portfolio case, the blazer slung over her arm and her sleeveless black silk blouse. Sighing in relief, she wiggled her stocking clad toes against the warm pavement. At least in September it was still safe to do this…no one was looking down anyway. She spared a glance at the oversized men's watch strapped to her petite wrist and winced.

Definitely go time.

Even at this early hour, the sun beating down on the pavement made each step feel like running on hot coals. The stretches of shade created by the towering buildings lining the street felt like heaven in comparison as she weaved through others making their own Monday morning trek. It became a game of darting from one shaded oasis to another. In patchier areas, it reminded her of skipping stones across a creek bed—a distraction to make the blocks fly by.

This job dropped in her lap. One lucky break in the shit storm that had carried away the house of cards that had been her life. Briar failed at being perfect in so many ways and lost everyone because of it, until Ann and Gigi opened this door for her. That's why she'd do much more than race down the sidewalk in her stalking feet—like she was now—to keep this job and earn the reset button her friends had given her. Allowing the rhythm of her pounding footsteps to take over like the second skin it had been back in her college days was a relief—pencil skirt be damned.

Racing the clock or another athlete was all the same to Briar. It fed her soul. Just what she needed on the first day if she was going to survive this and the struggles coming. For today, her finish line would be the shining glass building up ahead, like a towering beacon glowing for her in the morning light.

Briar skidded to a halt just a handful of steps from the gold lettered doors with a quarter hour to spare. Dropping the shoes on the sidewalk in front of her, she righted them with a pointed toe, slipped into their leather prison, and continued moving, albeit at a more appropriate pace. Pushing the door open, she remembered the blazer she'd carried due to the heat—crap. She brought the damn thing to cover her ink and combat the air-conditioned nightmare plaguing most office buildings. Was it so hard to pick a temperature below furnace and above refrigerator?

She started with her inked arm, sliding it in the sleeve while still clutching her leather portfolio case and planner to her chest. Better to hide the elaborate demon half-sleeve tattoo on her left arm and shoulder. She loved the still healing ink that Declan hooked her up with. It represented the evil weighing down the first half of her life. It wasn't her first ink but it was her best to date. Beautiful but not office appropriate, at least not until she scoped out the natives and checked the dress code policy.

Sliding her other arm into the blazer proved more of a challenge while still moving. She shifted her belongings to her now covered arm and reached back with the still bare arm to stick her hand in the sleeve. She ended up moving in a circle, like a dog chasing her tale. That's when she lost her grip and her portfolio slid out of her grasp and scattered across the marble tile floor.

Briar glanced up at the reception desk. A young blonde woman stood up behind the imposing mahogany desk with its wide granite counter. Her French manicured nails covered her mouth to hide the girly giggle and snort that would have been more at home coming from a 10-year-old girl. The smile in her eyes gave the receptionist away. Briar gave her a weak smile, straightened, and finished putting on her jacket—nothing out of the ordinary here. Just a twenty-something former collegiate star losing her shit.

Taking a deep steadying breath, she knelt down and began scooping her papers toward her and stacking them to put back in the leather folder. When she reached for one paper that had straggled further than the others, she heard it. The sound of fabric giving under the stress of her antics was not terribly different from the sound of torn paper. The strain of her run through downtown and the added ice cream inches—don't judge, divorce is hard—meant her skirt couldn't handle even a little more pressure.

Closing her eyes, she reached back and felt along the slit in her pencil skirt. Yep—she extended it by another three very indecent inches. Now, she had ten minutes to report in and correct a serious wardrobe malfunction.

A noise caught somewhere between a surprised gasp and a strangled cough occurred behind her, a distinctly masculine pitch to the sound. Her spine straightened and she resumed the collection of her papers as if she wasn't aware of all the eyes watching her humiliation—epic failure of a good impression.

There was another cough; this time more like the man behind her was clearing his throat purposely to get her attention. "Do you need help, ma'am? You look a little...out of sorts."

Briar glanced up and did a double take. His blue eyes glowed with his amusement but they were damn fine eyes to go with that strong smooth jawline and neatly combed back hair. Metrosexual wasn't the word for what this man was. No, he was an altogether different kind of animal. Those sharp eyes were predatory, giving her the impression that he'd be just as at home leading a team onto a football field for victory as he would brokering a deal in the boardroom. As if that wasn't enough to melt the panties on the coldest ice queen, he rocked a crisp white shirt and skinny black tie with a gray suit that likely cost more than her car. He could have been an extra on *Mad Men*. If she wasn't still technically married, he could bend her over anywhere he wanted her—not that her soon-to-be ex-husband deserved her fidelity.

Silence was not her friend in this situation if she planned to save any face. "I dropped my portfolio. Afraid I'm running late." Her cheeks burned in what had to be a furious shade of red on her otherwise pale complexion.

He knelt down beside her. The heat of having him so near her, reaching past her to gather the last of her things, burned through the jacket that had caused the whole mess. Handsome and chivalrous. Then he leaned over and ruined it all with a handful of whispered words. "You might want to do something about your skirt too. I believe you're out of dress code."

Instantly she went from fire to ice, although her cheeks were now likely stained purple from her level of embarrassment. She glared at the floor—anywhere really but the gorgeous man who choose now to point out her accident as if she'd already done something wrong. Didn't he know it wasn't polite to point it out?

They both stood, and he held out the last of her papers, neatly aligned. His hand slid over hers in the exchange—and unnecessary. Still, it thawed a little of the ice from his words. He probably thought he was being helpful or flirty. He looked too perfect. The nameless hot executive had to have some kind of flaw. Maybe his was overstating the obvious or an inability to talk to women. She should cut him some slack because that simple touch felt more purposeful than casual. It caressed her somewhere other than her hand and a long forgotten thrill coursing through her—the most action she'd seen in months.

He rested his hand over hers for a moment and continued in that same overly intimate whisper, "The ladies' room is just past the elevators."

Briar kept her eyes cast down, mumbling out her thanks. How had her life come to this? Turned on by a stranger pointing out where the damn bathrooms are located because of a wardrobe debacle—one that had officially made her late to work for the first time in her adult life.

She backed away a few steps, letting her eyes casually slide up, figuring she'd at least get a retreating view of him. Instead, he stood there watching her rather than move on with his day. That look in his eyes—crap, just how much of her had he gotten to see when her skirt tore? She tossed him a weak smile and turned racing the direction he'd indicated with as much dignity as she could muster into a confident strut as if nothing had happened and prayed she was only showing a little leg. She couldn't bring herself to slink away as though she were ashamed of her own body. Her honed athletic machine had taken her all the way to the Olympic tryouts before her knee had given out. Although she didn't look again, she'd swear on a stack of whatever holy books you handed her that his eyes had watched her the whole way.

Ciaran Rand was one lucky bastard.

Reason number one: executive privilege—he had walls that he was now safely behind and a solid wood door with no viewing window. After the scene in the lobby, he needed them to hide the raging hard-on the leggy vixen had just given him. Every other office in this building had glass walls or was a cubical. As the CFO second only to his grandfather, who hadn't been to the office in over a year, he had privacy. Not enough that he'd beat off in his office. Oh no—she would be his new favorite fantasy tonight—but enough privacy that he could get himself under control before his assistant dropped in to brief him on his day. Jack would be here any minute. That should have been enough to put the beast back in the cage. It wasn't.

Reason number two: the Death Before Decaf coffee shop. Ciaran reclined in the leather chair and sipped from the steaming cup he brought back with him, hoping the burn of scalding liquid might get him under control. That was why he'd been down in the lobby. He'd run out to the coffee shop across the street. As usual, he'd been in the office hours before anyone else and needed the extra shot of expresso to jump-start the second half of his morning. The swill he made if forced to use the machine here would kill somebody. No thanks—he'd pay for the good stuff. A man had to have priorities. Which led him back to her.

Reason number three: the spectacle of the skirt incident had been no less than a gift from god. An opportunity. Had he not been running across the street for his java fix, he might have missed the whole fiasco. He might have missed his chance to hear the sultry honey of her voice when she answered him. He could have said anything to her. He should have asked her name. But what did he do? Self-possessed chump that he was, called her out on dress code like a sanctimonious asshole.

What he needed to do was find her and get a second chance. Not knowing who she was made that an issue. If she came for a meeting, he could have Jack find out. They had security footage. Ciaran drummed his fingers against his thigh. No—he wasn't going to do any of those things. He wasn't a stalker. He was the future of this company. Plans were in motion that were far bigger than him. He would not abuse his power to have a woman in his bed even if the very idea of her tight legs wrapped around his head still had him hard as a rock under the desk.

Ciaran moved the mouse on his desktop to wake it up and the instant message box from Jack popped up immediately.

Jack: Ready for your morning briefing? Or are you still waiting on your crack-juice to return your soul.

Fingers flying across the keys, he typed up the response but hesitated. He still needed to get himself under control before spending time with another human being. He gave up and let the message go.

Business Casual

Ciaran: You're just as addicted. Let's get this over with. Your cup is getting cold.

Just having someone in his office would probably be enough to take care of the control issue. If it didn't, he was behind a damn desk.

Two sharp knocks cracked against the door before it swung open. Jack marched in, eyes glued to his tablet. Man couldn't carry a notebook like a normal person. He saw it as an inefficient waste of effort. The tablet allowed him to update the calendar or anything else in real-time for both of them. These morning briefings were also inefficient for the same reasons. Ciaran tried pointing out that it was redundant since he was more than capable of reading his own calendar of appointments. This quirk was particular to Jack, but whatever. Ciaran's day ran smoothly and a man couldn't ask for much more in his position. Jack was a godsend.

Of course a new HR director would be too if she ever got here. Ciaran hadn't met her yet. Jack hired her while Ciaran had been out of state speaking to stockholders in the Chicago office. This was one of many duties that he had taken over for his grandfather without actually being handed the reigns of CEO.

"What do I need to know for today, Jack?"

His assistant leaned across the desk to snatch up his coffee and marched across the office to drop onto the ridiculous chesterfield that lined one wall of his office. Jack casually rested his ankle on his left knee and sipped from his coffee as he continued to focus on the hand held device that seemed to be his life. "You have the morning blocked off for the new HR director. When Briar Goodall makes it, I'll have IT get her set up and I'll bring her back. Then lunch followed by a teleconference. Last but not least, your grandfather's secretary sent over a dinner meeting with Monica Fitch."

"Christ really? Cancel that one and send the usually apology note and flowers. Clearly, I'll need to have another one of those conversations with the old man. This is not a fucking episode of *The Bachelor*—and if you find out he signed me up for that show again, I swear to Christ…"

A strangled feminine laugh cut through Ciaran's rant. Ciaran looked up and blinked slowly at an illusion of epic nightmare proportions. Was he so starved for a woman in his bed that his mind turned on him? Because not ten feet from his desk, standing in his own goddamned door stood reason number four that he was a lucky bastard. The woman he wanted didn't need to be found. She found him.

Her eyes were round and luminous, a crystalline gray, and they bored into him unblinking as though she felt the same shock—an echo of what rolled through him. On her, it looked more like a rabbit caught in a snare. She shifted on her feet as if fighting the urge to flee. An irrational part of him wanted to see her run again. It had been so unexpectedly beautiful the first time.

"Ah—Ms. Goodall. So glad you found us." Jack waved her in with the hand holding his tablet.

Oh holy fuck. He was wrong. So wrong. He was not a lucky bastard at all.

"I'm sorry I'm late." That same sexy melody.

Ciaran stared blankly too tongue-tied to say anything. He was never coming out from behind this desk if he had this reaction just to her voice. Jack gave him a sidelong glance with one raised questioning brow before he finally responded. "Yes, well you called ahead and you found us. No harm." Jack looked to Ciaran. "Briar Goodall, your new HR director. Brair, this is Ciaran Rand. You'll be reporting to him."

She shook her head slightly and stepped forward hand extended. Ciaran took it, her slim warm fingers sliding into his hand, her grip firm as their eyes met. What kind of a man did it make him that he immediately pictured her grip on another part of his anatomy. He needed to pull it together before the situation spun any further out of his control.

"All things considered, you showed up remarkably quickly. I think we can excuse a tardy for a wardrobe malfunction. I assume it's been corrected?" Oh fuck—Ciaran's mouth obviously showed up without his brain.

All of the color drained from her face for approximately twenty seconds as she released his hand and crossed the room in silence to join Jack on the chesterfield. Yeah, he'd want to get away from him too if he were in her place. What possessed him to say that to her? She took a deep breath and smoothed the back of her skirt as she sat, crossing her ankles like a charm school debutant. Jack on the other hand, shifted to give Ciaran a questioning glare as he typed furiously on his tablet.

Jack: Are you always this rude to new hires? What's wrong with you?

Briar licked her lips, and pressed them together, her cheeks regaining color in a deeper shade than before as she spoke. "Yes—the unfortunate incident. It's been handled."

Ciaran wanted to sink into a hole. If he had to hazard a guess, she probably felt similarly at this point. Jack was already looking between them, putting pieces together where there were none. If he didn't get himself and this damn situation under some kind of control he was going to be the butt of every piece of office gossip. He did not need this distraction. He needed her out of his office, not handed to him on a silver platter that he could never touch—and damn did he want to touch the silky stocking covered legs. He wanted to run his hands up their smooth length and pull her across his desk until she—enough. The lawsuit potential alone should be scaring him off this line of thought.

This was so bad. Five days in a working week. Five days trapped with her. Fuck.

Chapter 3

JACK LED BRIAR OUT INTO THE HALL, BUT THEY DIDN'T go far. In fact, they only crossed and walked to the corner before he stopped, which of course she wasn't prepared for. She walked right into his back. She took a step back and mumbled an apology—something she'd been doing frequently since she set foot in this building. The office they stood in front of had two glass walls and a clear view of both the cubicle village of office support staff and a direct view of Ciaran's office door.

What a nightmare.

The hot jerk from the lobby was her boss. How could she stare at his door all day wearing the skirt that had her in this mess? Briar shifted back and forth in her heels. She needed to move—any movement really, although running would have been better—to relieve the rising tension in her muscles.

Flipping on a light switch about made her jump out of her skin. Jack held the glass door open for her. "Here you go. You're new home away from home."

She stepped past him and turned in a tight circle, taking it all in—blank white walls, double monitors, and the dock for her laptop connection, beige, metal, and glass. It was all standard issue office. More importantly, it represented a clean slate. A place to remake herself—right after she fixed her skirt.

Jack cleared his throat. "I'm going to get your new laptop and the phone number to IT so you can start getting logged into everything. Need anything in the mean time?"

"Directions to the nearest bathroom," Briar smiled innocently.

She'd closed the gap at the top of the split with the only safety pin she could find in the bottom of her purse, but it would only hold for so long. She needed Ann and a little privacy to vent about this awful start to her morning.

"Back towards the elevators and hang a right. You can't miss them." Jack met her strained smile with a sympathetic one as he backed out the door and returning to his cubicle, wherever that was.

"Thanks," but she was talking to herself.

Leaving her portfolio and other papers on the corner of the new desk, she clutched her phone to her chest and made a beeline in the direction that Jack indicated. She was texting Ann before the bathroom door even swung closed.

**Briar: S.O.S. Ladies' room sixth floor to the left
of the elevators. Hurry!**

Briar chewed on her bottom lip as she watched the bubbles dance across the screen indicating Ann was already messaging her back.

Ann: Bad morning?

Briar: Do you have safety pins? Wardrobe emergency.

Ann: Be there in five.

That seemed like a lifetime to pace and imagine her fresh start do a tailspin down the toilet. Ciaran was an even bigger asshole on meeting him for a second time and now he was her boss. How could she be expected to sit across from him every day and not launch herself across the conference room table to rub herself all over him like a damn cat—wait, no.

Briar didn't want Ciaran Rand. She had enough close encounters with assholes for one life time. If she ever dipped her toe in the dating pool again, she wanted a nice guy—someone sweet like Gigi had in Roman.

She stopped pacing and leaned on the white quartz counters, facing herself in the mirror, taking her own measure. Clearly, she needed to get real with herself. Her flushed skin and dilated pupils were enough of a giveaway. She wanted something alright, or rather, someone. Shit, her whole body tingled.

If anyone could tell her what to do about this mess—Ann would. If Briar had learned anything about her new friend in the weeks since deciding to make the move down here, Ann came prepared for everything and was quick with an opinion and a plan. God bless planners, everyone should have one.

Briar leaned against the cold tile wall beside the last bathroom stall. She wanted to close her eyes but all she could see were Ciaran's eyes watching her. Navy, like dark placid water. They surprised her with what they expressed even though he didn't say the thoughts behind them—shock first of all and then heat. That scared her more than any of the rest.

The door gave up a soft squeal, as it swung open. "What took you so long?" Briar's voice was horse with all the emotions she was forcing herself to swallow.

Ann's eyes widened, eyebrows going up as she raised a small zipper pouch like a shield. "I'm sorry. I had to find my sewing kit. Safety pins can only do so much."

Briar turned to reveal her damaged skirt as Ann knelt down beside her. "How did you make it this long in that skirt!"

"A safety pin and a prayer. I couldn't stomach the idea of being anymore late."

"So how did it go? I mean other than the late thing."

"It's a total disaster. When my skirt split, this amazing guy—straight out of *Mad Men*—I swear to God—he stopped to help me." Briar's mind drifted back to that moment—seeing him standing there—a sexy corporate titan at her rescue. She couldn't help but fan herself as she felt the flush creeping across her chest. "Then he ruined it with a snide comment about how I was out of dress code. I mean, really. Like I needed to hear that right at that moment."

Ann tugged at the fabric as she worked. "Wow, seriously?"

"That's not even the worst part. The hottie with the terrible verbal diarrhea, yeah—he's my boss." Briar craned her neck to look back at her friend as she spoke. "All along I've been dealing with Jack White and it turns out he's the executive assistant. I never would have guessed that I reported directly to the CFO."

Ann swatted her leg and spoke through teeth clenched around a needle. "Hold still." She removed her tiny bit of metal from her mouth and started to sew before she continued. "So he's a jerk huh? I've heard stories about Ciaran Rand being made of ice. But I've never had to run into the guy on my floor."

"Yeah, and he commented about how nice it was to see I was back in dress code and that he could forgive me being late in light of the circumstances."

"How magnanimous of him." The implied eye roll dripped from her voice.

"That's the thing. Seeing how he watched me, holy cow—smoldering is an understatement. He looked like he wanted to follow me into the bathroom he directed me to and I might have let him if he hadn't been such an ass. God that sounds awful doesn't it. It just doesn't add up. If he's interested, why is he acting like a jerk?"

"Makes sense to me. Now he knows you're his employee and doesn't want to get in trouble for saying something inappropriate to the HR Director of all people. Don't forget that's who you are now. The last thing that man needs is a sexual harassment charge within his own company."

Briar shook her head, but Ann's assessment loosened the knot in her stomach by several degrees. "He has nothing to worry about. Regardless of what my hormones want, I'm not ready to date, and if I was, it wouldn't be someone I work with."

"Hey, there's nothing wrong with that." In the mirror, Briar could see Ann's chin dip down, hiding her face.

"Which part?" Briar's eyebrows went up at the red creeping up her friend's neck. "Are you having a little extracurricular activity at work?"

"Maybe." Ann's voice was small, like she wasn't necessarily proud of herself. That didn't sit well with what Briar knew of Ann.

Briar kept her own voice even, doing her best not to let any judgment leak in, especially considering how supportive Ann had been with nothing more than Gigi to recommend Briar as a friend. "I thought I heard there was something going on with you and Declan?"

"That would be my brother and soon-to-be sister-in-law meddling. I know she was your roommate and she has the best intentions." Ann sat back on her heels and tugged at the Peter Pan collar of her high-necked blouse before resuming her sewing efforts. "She's my best friend and I practically handpicked her to be my sister-in-law, but there's history she doesn't know about. I just—I can't go back. He's a great guy. He deserves a great girl. I'm just not her."

"So office fraternization isn't against the rules here."

"Well you know—we keep it on the down low. The guy isn't my boss. He's in another department but we're colleagues. He does have the potential to be my boss someday." Then Ann smiled, a bit of that cocky confidence shining back through. "That won't happen. I'll get there first, of course."

Briar met the reflection of Ann's eyes in the mirror. "Was there ever a doubt?"

Ann swatted Briar's butt and she let out a soft yelp of surprise making them both laugh. "There. That's the best I can do. Don't do any crazy bending or anything like that, but it should hold you to the end of the workday."

Briar turned her back to the mirror and looked over her shoulder to inspect the skirt. "Thank you. You're such a lifesaver. It amazes me that you're so prepared."

"Don't mention it. You'll get me back at some point." Ann winked and then disappeared out the ladies' room door to wherever in this building her office happened to be.

Ann's confession got her thinking, was it true that the fraternization here is really no big deal? Because my God—Ciaran Rand—of all the things that could've woken up her desire to be touched, he should not be it. She should block it from her mind. Her husband hadn't even shown his face to be served with the divorce papers. At least when that happens, she could feel a lot better about it—not that she should feel any guilt at all.

Procrastination wasn't going to get her through this day. She needed to get back to her desk and get setup. At the very least, she could drown herself in work. There had to be a project somewhere on her calendar that she could sink her teeth into.

Briar washed her hands for good measure and pushed the door open to head back out. She strode down the hall toward her new office with confidence she'd been faking before Ann's intervention. All of which came to a heart stuttering halt at the sight of Ciaran standing outside her door speaking to Jack.

It didn't stop her though. She looked up at him through her lashes, head down as she mumbled, "Excuse me gentleman."

They stepped back to allow her past. Jack gave her plenty of room, but Ciaran gave her just enough. Not touching, but so close that the strange charge between them had no trouble making the leap. She forced down the full body shudder crawling up her spine—not an icky feeling at all. Oh no, this was delicious and she was only on Monday. Dear God, this was going to be a long week if she couldn't get a handle on these hormones. Judging from the banked heat in Ciaran's eyes and the way he clenched his fist at his side—the side facing away from Jack—he felt it too. Oh boy.

Chapter 4

THREADING THROUGH THE RAMBLING STREAM OF business professionals funneling up the sidewalk, Briar moved with the light step of someone on time—and damn, did that make today better than yesterday. The commute was easier for one. She'd even managed a parking spot on the first attempt.

Her cell phone vibrated inside her purse as her building came in sight. She slid the device from her bag and swiped at the screen without looking to see who it was. Only a handful of people had her number anyway.

Before she could even get out the required hello, Todd's shrill tenor—a weird hybrid of growl and whine—blared through the line. "Who are these people living in my house and why are the fucking locks changed? What did you do?"

"If I were you, I would leave before someone calls the

cops. Trespassing is illegal." Briar couldn't help the satisfied smile that tugged up the corners of her mouth. It put an extra bounce in her step. "It's not your house. It never was—and I sold it."

She heard a car door slam on the other end of the line. "Why did you sell our house?"

"Why did you fuck my mother?" She shot back at him. Clearly he only heard the parts he wanted to hear, like usual.

Todd's tone softened, cajoling. "Come on baby. Don't be like that. You know I love you."

She disconnected the call. The days where that still excused his behavior were over and she had shit to do—like work.

Briar pushed the gleaming glass door of her office building with her hip as she scrolled through her contact list and gave a jaunty little wave to the snooty receptionist as she passed on her way to the elevators. Her phone rang again in her hand. She sent Todd's call straight to voicemail as she pulled up her private investigator's phone number and hit dial.

After two rings, the line connected and a gruff male voice came on the line. "What can I do for you, Ms. Goodall?" At least one of them used the caller ID.

"Todd's back in town. Can you get him and serve the papers? I want this divorce finished." She stepped onto the elevator, smiling politely at the other people entering with her.

"And just how do you know that little lady?"

"Because he just called me and asked about people living in the house I sold a month ago. Do me a favor and get to it fast please." She kept her voice low and smile firmly in place.

"Consider it done."

The line disconnected and she scrolled through her contacts looking for the next number she needed, her lawyer. She hit send and let it ring. She needed to act fast or Todd would be gone again. He was likely on his way to the bank and their empty accounts.

This time she got voicemail. "Jay, I think we got him. I'll let you know for sure when I get the confirmation from the contact you referred me to. Todd called me; he's back in St. Cloud."

She ended the call as the elevator doors opened. She stepped out, her head down, searching for the next number she needed and right into the arms of her boss.

Ciaran's hands closed around her arms, steadying her. Oh my—he smelled good—like warm leather and aftershave. She should not be having these kinds of thoughts about her boss. But damn she couldn't help the urge to rub her face against him like a cat. Briar took a deep steadying breath and stepped back out of his grip.

"I'm so sorry. I really should've paid more attention to where I was going instead of getting wrapped up in a phone call." Heat flushed her cheeks as she spoke and his hands dropped from her.

Was that a smile on Rand's face? Oh, my God, he was smiling at her and it was a damn nice smile. A Michael Fassbender kind of smile, you know, the hotness that played Mr. Rochester in that new version of *Jane Eyre* that she practically watched on auto repeat on her bad days. He smiled in that roguish kind of way that set her on fire. If she were Jane, she'd never have run away—never mind that he had a crazy wife in the attic. She would absolutely have lived in sin. It was also highly unprofessional to be standing here having these thoughts. That needed to stop now.

"Briar—my office, coffee in five minutes." His eyes slid over her and then quickly away, as his deep voice snapped out the command. He stepped to the side away, unblocking her path and continued toward his office.

Just like that. No good morning. No hello—just giving an order and walking away. She sighed in exasperation. At least he didn't say something rude this time.

As the thought flitted through, from behind her, his voice broke through the lusty mire that already had her prepared to forgive him for his abruptness.

"And, Briar? You're out of dress code."

What the actual fuck?

Briar looked down at herself as she hurried past rows of cubicles toward her glass-walled office she thought of as the fishbowl. She was not out of dress code. This was a perfectly respectable skirt. Yes, the pencil skirt was above the knee, but there was no rule against that. She should know—she spent half her evening with a gin and tonic in one hand and the policy handbook queued up on her tablet in the other. It couldn't be her tattoos. They weren't offensive in image or language, per the rules she read. Even if they were, they were covered up—at least for today.

This would grate at her nerves until she routed out the deficiency and corrected it. Her skin prickled with heat and she was at least ninety percent sure that if she looked down at her chest she would be splotchy with hives—stress had a way of doing that to her. This was only day two. If she felt this way now, how bad would it be in a month? Couple that with her suddenly raging hormones over her boss—an unfortunately hot asshole—and she was living a recipe for disaster.

Briar reached her office, dropped her belongings on the desk, closed the door then the blinds, cutting off access to everyone watching her. They were likely too busy with their tasks to pay any attention to her, but it didn't take away the feeling of eyes on her.

How many minutes did she have left? Briar lifted her arm to look at the man's watch strapped to her wrist—three minutes. Fuck it, she would be late. In fact, fuck it might become her new mantra at her current rate. Briar refocused on her cell phone and its web browser to make one last call. It didn't take long to pull up the phone number to the bank that held Todd's car loan.

It took two precious minutes of hold time to get an actual person on the line—minutes that she needed to get to Ciaran's office and solve her wardrobe mystery. She gave the banker with the slow southern drawl the quick rundown of where she expected they could find Todd and the car.

Briar received the notice to cure default just last week. It was his name on the loan, not hers, but she was listed as a contact reference. She stopped making his car payments the day he moved out and apparently, he never started paying them. Why the douche assumed she would continue to carry him was beyond her comprehension. Then again, the idiot called her baby as if she hadn't caught him in the act of cheating in their bed. It was the first item she burned before selling the house.

Satisfied with her small vengeful act—she grabbed her

notebook, her favorite gel pen, and her laptop. Her phone was still in her hand as she headed for Rand's office.

Ciaran frowned at her as she entered the office, but she also noticed the way his eyes tracked her as he listened to Jack ramble on about one of their projects. Somehow, the downturned corners of his mouth was sexier than his earlier smile.

"I said five minutes, Briar. So nice of you to finally join us." If he'd been a snake, his voice would have dripped irritation like venom.

Jack gave her an apologetic smile, as if embarrassed by his boss's attitude, but as far as she could see this was perfectly normal behavior since she'd met Ciaran Rand. Why should Jack be fazed when it didn't bother her?

Ciaran gestured towards the cabinets against the wall. He continued with the conversation, he'd been having with Jack, which sounded like nothing more than a general rundown of the schedule for the day.

One steaming cup remained waiting in the tray, bearing the logo of the coffee shop across the street, Death Before Decaf. An assortment of single serve creamers and sweeteners laid spread out for her. She quickly doctored her coffee, cleaned up after herself and returned to the group.

Since Jack had already claimed the one empty chair across from Rand's desk, Briar took the couch along the opposite wall. She set her cup down on the coffee table, giving him a brief glimpse of her cleavage. She could lie and say it wasn't on purpose, but she did like the little thrill it gave her to tease him. While she didn't plan to pursue whatever might be happening, it didn't mean she couldn't at least innocently enjoy the flirtation. There was also no harm in lying to herself. She smoothed her skirt as she sat, crossing her legs to balance her notebook on her knee, her laptop open on the arm of the sofa beside her.

She waited for a break in conversation before she interjected. "I apologize for being late. Can someone bring me up to speed on what's happening?

Watching Briar perched in the corner of his sofa, beautiful long legs crossed, made Ciaran's fingers twitch with the need to come out from behind this desk and run his hands over the black lines of her stocking covered calves. His mouth watered with the wholly inappropriate need to taste her. He licked his lips and instead lifted his coffee, taking one scalding sip. Coffee was fine but she would taste better.

This line of thought had to stop. He needed control. There couldn't be a relationship between them—why the word even entered his mind should send a chill straight through him. He never wanted or needed one before. Even if he reconsidered that position, now was not the time. Not with his goal in its current uncertain state. Briar was his employee and if he didn't stop, a sexual harassment lawsuit was waiting to happen.

Dammit—for the first time, he almost didn't care. That's what finally struck him with any kind of self-preserving caution, and at this rate even that might not hold.

Jack cleared his throat, eyebrows raised expectantly waiting for Ciaran to take control and fill in the blank of Briar's question.

"The expectation is that every morning you'll come to my office for briefing on the day. Since you're in training and you and I will be working fairly close, Jack will be handling both of our schedules. It's easier for him to fill us in once."

"No problem, I can handle that. Friday, however, I will have to miss our briefing. I have an appointment with my lawyer."

Jack tapped his stylus on the desk like a tiny gavel to interject. "Would you like me to start from the top?"

Briar opened her kissable red lips to answer but Ciaran jumped in. "Not today. She'll be with me most of the day working on the new policy handbook. We can let you carry on with your day I think."

It probably was not the best move to be alone with her, but Ciaran couldn't resist the opportunity. Jack gave Ciaran a sideways look but held his tongue. Collecting his coffee and precious tablet, he smiled at her and winked, leaving Ciaran with a sudden urge to fire his longtime assistant—a man he knew he could never replace.

Jack stopped in front of her on his way out and leaned in, but his conspiratorial whisper still carried. "His bark is worse than his bite. Don't let this thug intimidate you." Jack straightened. "Holler if you need me."

He left the room, shutting the door behind him. Shutting them in together.

"So now can we discuss what in particular I'm wearing that offends you?" The look on her face as she asked the question, the affronted dignity and irritation, and more than that, her tone and the word choice were a challenge.

Ciaran had forgotten. He was too busy being consumed in the details of her and having her alone. The infraction was small and frankly it turned him on to see, as much as her reaction and resulting challenge had. He couldn't let himself have her, but damn was it fun to get under her skin. He made the comment and now he had to answer for it.

"Fishnets." He allowed his gaze to glide up the offending article of hosiery. "They have a certain unprofessional connotation that falls outside the bounds of business casual. Not quite polished enough for the Rand Enterprises look."

Her dark eyes flashed like black ice, the cold danger that if you ignored could spin you out of control. It was too late for him—he already had. But the silence. That was the most telling feature of her mood. She opened her mouth as if to say something, stopped, as though weighing her words, and then started again.

Ciaran picket up his laptop and moved to join her on the sofa. Dangerous to sit so close to her—and not because of the possibility of frostbite—but he couldn't help himself, couldn't stay away from her any longer. She was magnetic.

"Did you read the policy handbook yesterday?" Ciaran kept his eyes on his screen, but felt hers boring into him as if she were waiting for something else.

"I took notes, but I don't recall anything in the dress code about fishnets."

Shots fired—good. He would have hated her to be the kind of woman who just bent to someone else's will.

Somehow, he'd known she had that kind of quiet strength, like tempered steel. She at least would make the workday interesting.

"It's implied. Nothing worn and informal, too revealing or to sheer. If those terms don't satisfy you, than manager discretion. If we listed every article of clothing specifically, we'd have a novel just on dress code."

The regular irritated staccato of Briar's pen on the edge of her notepad stilled, as the corners of her red painted lips turned down. "Manager Discretion is a cop out. I pegged you better than that."

"To be fair, it wasn't my first point. Now can we move on or do we need to start with that policy for the actual work to begin?" Ciaran glanced down at his watch. "I have a meeting in two hours and I would like to have this drafted for review by the end of the week."

She leaned forward to grab her coffee off the table, scooting closer to Ciaran, until her knee brushed his. His body reacted to her immediately. A small innocent accident forced him to cover the evidence of her effect on him with a laptop that was not really up for the task. Her grip on the cup tightened and she glanced first at their touching knees and then up at Ciaran as if expecting him to move or say something snide.

He sat frozen in the snare of her dilated pupils, locked on his, which likely were just as bad, and the pink flush of heat gracing her soft cheeks and the swell of her breasts. Not focusing on that alone was a struggle. Damn, when she leaned over the table earlier, he nearly choked on his coffee.

"Sorry. Where would you like to start? I have a list of

policies I think should be added. I noticed you're lacking one on social media for instance. I also didn't see anything on nepotism and fraternization. Although, considering Rand Enterprises is owned and run your family, I understand why you don't have one in here."

And just like that he could see why Jack hired her. Briar saw straight to the point. She was perfect for him. He shook the thought lose. *She's perfect for Human Resources.* Ciaran cleared his throat. "Let's start with existing policies; although I agree. We will have to address those topics. That's why this needs to happen."

Her eyes stayed down on her notepad as she sipped her coffee, but over the edge of the cup, Ciaran could see the faint hint of a smile at his small praise of her. It was a lovely smile and he wanted more of it. Another sign of what a long week this was about to be.

Chapter 5

RUNNING FELT CATHARTIC AFTER A LONG DAY
of her hormones on overdrive and it was only Tuesday. This never stopped being Briar's favorite escape—meditative even. The oppressive heat of a summer that refused to acknowledge football season had started and the leaves that should be changing, didn't put her off. The rhythm of each step pounding against the pavement, the vibrations rippling through her muscles, as oxygen burned through her limbs. The sound of her own breathing—these became a focus to carry away her concerns. The only missing piece was the thrill of competition with its adrenaline high, to make this feeling complete.

She needed every second of this to burn a man out of her thoughts and for the first time in months, she didn't mean her soon-to-be ex-husband. Ciaran was an abrasive ass and noticed everything. Except her. But he did watch her. She would be typing up a section they just discussed and feel his gaze. Their eyes would connect, and every time the steel fire in his eyes made her breath catch. Then he'd look away. Sometimes in meetings she'd catch him while someone else was presenting. Did he expect her to say something and she let him down? Or was it something more happening?

Briar did respect the hell out of Ciaran. He seemed to have a progressive attitude as they worked through policy after policy. Often, he embraced progressive ideas while other corporations of their longevity seamed to cling to the status quo with an iron grip. Then, the man's work ethic—she understood from Jack that he came in hours before all the rest of them. When she left for the night he was still at it. He worked like a man possessed— like he had a passion for his business that she longed to feel for anything.

Slowing, she found a shady spot and took her pulse. She needed to refocus. She had more than she could have asked for with the oppressive humidity. The sun was bright, the leaves were still green and she was going to be a free woman— eventually, now that the papers were being served.

She'd been trying different areas for a good place to run. Most of the parks so far seemed crowded with play equipment and kids. Not so with this one. Those things were here but there were trails available that weren't so bad and the drive from the apartment had been short. She might even walk the distance as a warm up.

Briar set off again but made it two steps before she heard the bikes coming up behind her. She moved to the right to let them pass. The first flew past. The second swerved over and knocked into her.

She stumbled back into a tree but didn't manage to catch herself in time to keep from tumbling into the smaller thorny vegetation beside it.

The bicyclist called back to her. "Get out of the way, lady!"

That asshat had the gall to blame her. "Fuck you," she yelled back.

Briar laid there, seething. This was just like the rest of her life. She made way for others and not once did anyone have the decency to make room for her—even on a common park trail. When was it her turn?

Soft footfalls crunching the dirt path shook her free from her pity party. Time to get up before whomever this was found her laying here and had her ass committed, because she had to look crazy laying here sweaty and cursing for no good reason.

The tug of a branch pulled the shoulder strap of her tank, catching on the exposed strap of her sports bra as she moved to sit up. It dragged against her skin. "Shit. That hurts." She reached to free herself but the strain on the fabric only got worse as she twisted to free herself.

"Need help?"

"I need assholes on mountain bikes to watch where the fuck they're going."

A deep chuckle caressed her skin. Then his voice registered through her frustration. She pulled harder to free herself as her cheeks burned. Why now? Why, when she should have been in her element, did he have to see her now? The universe clearly had it out for her.

"I can see that. Let me help you up."

"No that's okay. I got it." Then the fabric gave with a pop

that snapped against her skin, then fell lax—too loose not to be exposing more flesh then she would have liked. She dropped her head to hide her face. "Shit."

Briar turned her eyes up to Ciaran's amused face. She gripped the torn edge of her shoulder straps, holding them up and herself in.

"What's with you and tearing your clothes? It's like you're trying to flash me. Don't you think we should know each other better first?" He held out his hand to her.

Laughter bubbled up. The whole thing was so ridiculous she couldn't help it. He was kind of right. If she was going to flash him this often—it was her second time in as many days so she couldn't argue the trend—she really should get to know him. It helped that this time he made a joke instead of being an asshole. Or was she just so keyed up before that she'd mistaken humor for a dick move? Either way the man was right.

She slid her free hand—the one not keeping her breast securely covered—in his outstretched hand. His fingers were warm and rougher than she expected for someone so well groomed, a dyed in the wool metrosexual. Maybe it was part of his hidden depths that she should get to know, kind of like the dry humor. He hauled her easily to her feet, pulling her until her body bumped against his, her covered breasts rubbing against his cotton T-shirt.

Ciaran looked damn good in a sleeveless shirt with its collar cut out to be more open. But the feel of his hard body underneath rubbing against hers, even for that unintentional millisecond, had her hot and bothered, more than an afternoon of running could hide. He released her hand and whipped off the aforementioned shirt.

"Here. I can run around topless and no one's going to say anything." He held the gray shirt out to her that she'd been having indecent thoughts about seconds before.

"Thanks. Nice to know chivalry isn't dead." She took it and clutched it to her chest for a moment.

A T-shirt covered in man sweat should be grossing her out. She should pass it back, not put it on. Instead, as she slid it over her head she took a deep breathe. Mmh—she'd forgotten how good a man could smell. Earthy but not in a dirty way, more like juniper or something a little evergreen and spicy. At least he couldn't see her face in that split second of reaction. There was no hiding that lust but at least the rising flush in her skin could be explained away as embarrassment.

Until the t-shirt hit the back of her knees, she had no idea just how big of a man Ciaran was. Or for the love of god—just how cut he looked under that suit. This man ran often, and probably lifted weights because you didn't get that kind of definition otherwise. She a clear mental image formed of him on a chin up bar pulling himself up with bulging arms and flexing pecks. Her fingers twitch with involuntary need to trace their curve down the centerline of his abs. Then her eyes found the start of his V where his basketball shorts hung low on his hips.

Briars eye's bounced up to meet Ciaran's and her cheeks burned brighter with his knowing smile. She'd been caught.

"Run here often?" Great now her voice was coming out sultry, like a cat in heat.

"I was about to ask you the same."

She shook her head. "I've been feeling out the trails for a good place to run. First time on this one since I moved here."

"Mind if I keep you company today?"

"Well there is that matter of getting to know me before I bare it all." Gigi would be proud of her for that one—not that Briar should be flirting. This may not be work, but since the man was still her boss, accidental run-in/rescue only carried her so far.

He smiled and his hand fell to the small of her back, ushering her back into motion at an easy pace and she let him. Her flesh beneath his hand tingled, as though her skin absorbed his energy right through the cotton.

"Can we start over? I feel like I got such a bad start and you've only seen me in the worst light possible."

"I don't know about that. You look like grace under pressure to me."

She felt the compliment all the way to the tips of her toes. When was the last time a man said something like that to her? "I'm not generally a late person, I've never been a klutz until I've been around you, and the last time I cursed like that I tore my meniscus."

"That's a hell of an injury to come back from. Like I said grace under pressure. Not many others would get back to the trails. How long ago?"

Briar smiled at his interest. "Junior year of college. I was prepping for the Olympic trials. I'd won nationals and even though my coach advised against it, I was working myself hard to get ready. I learned to listen after that."

"Cross country or sprints? What was your event?"

"Both but for the Olympics, I was going for the 100 meter dash. I miss it."

"I'm sure that you do. To compete on that level takes

passion and commitment that most people don't have."

Briar could feel the blush creeping up her neck with all the compliments. She would be surprised if she didn't have hives on her chest at this point. She had to get the topic off herself fast and cool down.

"Did you do track or is this just a workout for you?"

"Just a workout. I did amateur boxing much to my grandfather's chagrin. My mom used to tell me stories of her father and grandfather boxing in Ireland. When I asked, she let me. The look on my grandfather's face the first time I came for a visit with a black eye is something I will never forget. Bless my mom, she wouldn't back down and pull me out when he demanded it. Said his heir would not be a bruiser."

"I know what you mean. My mom hated that I was a runner. Said it was fine as a hobby to help me keep my figure but it would never get me a husband. Dad made her back off and when we lost him I was old enough to fight for myself and stay in it."

Although he faced the path ahead of them, his gaze seemed unfocused as he asked in a hushed voice, "How old were you?"

"Sixteen," she answered, chocking back the burn of tears that threatened. It had been so long since she'd even turned her mind to it. "Got hit by a drunk driver coming home from the office."

"I lost Mom at seventeen to cancer. Dad was pretty much a mess after that. Left me to my grandfather to lick his wounds. Can't say I blame him. She left a pretty big hole in all of us."

"She sounds like she was a wonderful person." She couldn't help the reverent awe in her tone. Not many people could identify with that part of her past—losing a parent—she certainly wouldn't wish it on anyone. The shared connection was unexpected but welcome.

"She was. She's the reason I'm next in line for CEO of Rand. My father loved her so deeply that when my grandfather forbid them to marry, my Dad gave it all up and went into business for himself. When I was born, my grandfather settled it all on me and started grooming me to take my place as soon as I could read and count to ten."

"Sounds like he would get along with my mother. You know that show *Toddlers and Tiaras* with the pageant kids? I was one of those kids until I begged my father to make her stop. Not literally on the show, but I did the pageant circuit."

Gigi didn't even know that. Those pictures were hidden away and as long as no one knew, even the internet wouldn't out her to her friends. Telling him went against the grain but not many people understood the connection of losing a parent and the strain of pleasing the family you have left.

"No shit?" He gawked at her, eyes raking her body as they moved.

"Pageant queen and terror on the track. I've got hidden depths." She wiggled her eyebrows suggestively, which elicited another laugh—a sound that she was starting to crave thanks to the gratifying chill it sent to all her lady parts.

They came to the end of the trail and the row of parked cars. Instead of relief to be out of his company and free, she felt a pang of regret. She'd enjoyed getting to see this side of him, to relate with him almost as much as she enjoyed getting a sidelong view of him running beside her naked from the waist up.

"Which one is yours?"

She pointed across the lot to her Challenger, glowing like blue fire in the sun. "The Dodge beside that black sedan."

"I parked by you."

"That boring thing is yours." Briar slapped her hand over her mouth. Shit that was rude. "I just mean you have such good taste in suits. You can't tell me you couldn't do better than that?" Dammit. She cringed at herself. That was almost worse.

Again, the warm rich sound of his laughter dissipating her worry over the faux pas. "I like you when you don't filter. You're right. It's boring like me. I bought it for the safety rating and gas mileage. Yours on the other hand, suits you now that I know you're a beauty queen that likes to go fast."

Briar leaned one hip against the rear quarter panel of her car and gripped the door handle in one hand, still facing Ciaran. "You don't strike me as someone who plays it safe. A bit of a stickler for the rules—sure. That comes with the territory of a good leader, but I think you're more of a calculated risk taker. Makes me want to ruffle your feathers a little."

He reached up, his hand caressing her cheek as he tucked an errant strand of hair that somehow came loose from her top knot. The touch was innocent on the outside but considering he was her boss, he shouldn't be touching her at all. "Believe me, you are already."

Oh, shit. What did that mean? Her body knew what it wanted such a bold statement to mean, but her heart and her common sense were quaking in their proverbial boots. It wasn't technically a blatant come on. Did she encourage him or play it cool? Did she want that from him? She wasn't divorced yet and he was her boss. Hell—she hardly knew him. She could at least admit she wanted that—to know him on a level that went past boss and employee or even past coworker.

Briar played the middle road. "Thank you for keeping me company. I promise I'll try to keep my clothes on tomorrow."

His lips spread into a crooked smile that made him look like a romance novel cover model before he leaned in, his lips so close to her cheek she could feel the heat of his breath on her skin and smell the spice in his aftershave. "Don't stay dressed on my account."

Those whispered words sent heat flooding through Briar and her nipples tingled in response. She leaned against the car for support, completely struck dumb. It left her no choice but to stand there and watch as he strolled to his sedate black Audi that she suddenly wanted to check out the backseat of. She didn't move until he'd driven away with a small wave through his darkened windows.

Thud, thud, thud. "We come bearing ice cream!" Gigi's voice carried through the door in a singsong rhythm. "Open up. I know you're in there. You don't get to sit at home alone wallowing."

Briar padded across the floor as she wound her hair up in a towel to dry, no doubt leaving a trail of drips and wet footprints in her wake. She hadn't exactly been wallowing, more like drowning out her hormones under the hot spray of her shower after her run with Ciaran. Somehow, she had to rinse all her new dirty thoughts right down the drain. Hell, she sang the damn song from *South Pacific* like it was her anthem through her whole shower.

As she swung the door open, she caught the tail end of Ann berating Gigi in an exasperated whisper. "I can't believe you didn't keep a copy of the key? We could be walking in there right now. What if she was sick or…" Ann stopped and turned her head slowly towards Briar, her hazel eyes wide with false innocence. "Hi. How long have you been standing there with the door open?"

Leaning against the casement, Briar scrunched her face up in a mockery of stern disappointment. "Long enough to hear you suggest that you're totally okay with a little breaking and entering under the guise of my safety."

The aghast look of horror that spread across Ann's face made it impossible to hold her own stern expression together for more than thirty seconds before Briar lost it in a fit of the giggles that Gigi had already caved to.

Ann crossed her arms under her breasts, a fabric grocery bag dangling from one hand. "And to think I brought shit to share. I see how you bitches operate."

This sparked another fit until Briar dabbed at the happy tears burning the corners of her eyes and took several deep breathes. "Get your asses in here. I totally needed that." She stepped back to let them enter and then closed the door behind them.

"I know. That's why we're here. Jay called." Gigi traipsed straight to the kitchen and made herself at home—which it technically still was—unloading the contents of her own rose print grocery bag. Only Gigi would turn something so mundane into another pink fashion accessory.

"So much for lawyer-client privilege," Briar mumbled.

Gigi shrugged. "What can I say, sisterly benefits." Her former roommate held up a pint and waved it in encouragement. "Dark chocolate or milk chocolate with caramel?"

Ann's nose scrunched up in disgust. "Neither; no one is interested in your dairy-free crap. She's having an adult root beer float with me."

Using the pint to gesture, Gigi pointed at her, waving it up and down as she vented her conviction over her healthy treat. "I've got a wedding dress to fit into. You shouldn't knock it before you try it. The almond milk ice cream tastes kinda like toasted almond fudge. And I didn't ask you, Ann. I asked her." She pointed to Briar as if they needed a visual reminder of who she was referring to.

"What's this adult root beer float?" Briar asked, cutting off the bickering before it could go any further.

Ann smiled; her grin carried a distinct note of gloating victory. "Alcoholic root beer and vanilla ice cream."

Apparently well-deserved gloating. The better Briar got to know Ann the more she liked her. "Sorry, Gigi. After the day I've had, alcohol-laced ice cream sounds like heaven. I'll get the cups. Spoons are in the drawer next to the fridge."

Pumping her fist in victory, Ann spun around and grabbed three spoons from the drawer, passing one to Gigi who grabbed it from her hand as she reached around her to pop the unneeded pint into the freezer. Gigi yanked the top off the remaining pint and speared the contents with her spoon. Then she hoisted herself up onto the counter, crossing her legs at the ankle like somebody's five-year-old pretty pink princess eating pilfered ice cream. The scene unfolded like watching a low budget ballet.

Briar shook her head as she sat the cups on the counter and stepped back out of the way. The kitchen wasn't big enough for three grown ass women even if those two made it look effortless.

She caught her reflection in the glass of one of Gigi's picture frames, reminding her of the towel currently wound up on her head. "While you all are doing that, I'm going to finish my hair."

"Do you have foam rollers?" Gigi called after her.

"You are not doing my hair," Briar yelled back as she passed through the bedroom to get to the bathroom. At least the steam had a chance to clear.

"You're no fun." Gigi's voice became louder as she gave up her perch and followed Briar. "It could be like college. You looked fantastic with a wet set."

"Just because I have blonde hair and blue eyes doesn't mean I'm your live-action Barbie doll. Find a new victim." Briar pulled the now soaked towel from her hair and spread it out over the empty towel bar to dry out.

Ann appeared over Briar's shoulder in the mirror. "I chopped my hair off and died it blonde so that I could stop being her Christina."

"But you're my person," Briar protested.

"I don't even like *Gray's Anatomy.*"

Briar and Gigi turned, gasping in slack-jawed horror as Ann sat the red solo cup in front of Briar on the bathroom counter.

"I feel like I don't even know you right now." Briar stuck a spoon full of ice cream in her mouth as she continued to shake her head.

Turning to Gigi Briar said, "I thought you said we could trust her." She worked the brush through her hair. "You know, Ann, if you hadn't come here with ice cream and alcohol, I'm not even sure we could be friends."

"You two are ridiculous." Ann vacated the doorway and made herself comfortable on the edge of Gigi's former bed, covered in Briar's newly purchased silver and violet linens.

Much to Briar's surprise, Gigi's former bedroom lacked the vibrant colors she'd come to associate with her friend. Thankfully, she'd come prepared. In her boredom after the great purge, she indulged in a little online shopping. After all, she'd burned the linens right along with every sheet set and blanket in her house. There was no telling how long her mother had been sleeping with her husband or even how many other skanks there had been during their marriage, since he'd never shown much interest in her past the obligatory once a month missionary that required a blowjob from her to even get started.

It was little wonder her hormones were raging around Ciaran. Setting aside the enlightening conversation they'd had on her run, he may be an arrogant, insufferable prick, but from what she could see around the office, he gave the appearance of at least being fair and more often than not, generous. Jack explained at lunch that Ciaran did that coffee run every morning and they never had to chip in. If he was that generous to people he paid to employ, she could only imagine how he would be in a more intimate setting—something she really shouldn't do. It also didn't hurt that he oozed sex appeal through the seams of his overpriced suit.

Gigi milled around the bedroom behind her. "Start talking, Briar. Tell me about this sexy boss who calls you out on your wardrobe choices."

Briar poked her head out of the open bathroom door, glaring daggers at Ann. "Traitor."

She had the gall to play innocent and bat her eyelashes. "What? I figured you would have told her already. I was kind of surprised that I told her first considering how far back you all go."

"You only know because I needed you to save my ass," Briar called back out the bathroom door. She stuck her tongue out at herself in the mirror and then turned, leaning one hip against the doorframe as she continued to work on her hair. "Today he called me out on my fishnet tights. Gave me a bullshit cop-out about it being implied in the policy. He's a total ass, but a good looking one. At least I thought he was an ass until I ran into him on the trail during my run. He must live around here or something."

"Wait, you ran into him?" Gigi stopped in the middle of her pacing to focus on Briar.

She shrugged. "Yeah, and he behaved like a gentleman for a change."

"And?" Gigi gestured with her spoon, circling it as if she

could pull out more details.

"And nothing. I came home and took a shower, which you interrupted with ice cream and malt liquor masquerading as root beer. What's there to tell?"

"For you to say that, he clearly did more than smile and run on past. We want the dirt." Gigi abandoned her pint on the lowboy dresser and sauntered to the closet, flipping through the dresses.

Finished with her hair, Briar left her brush on the back of the toilet, grabbed the drink Ann left for her and took her first sip through the straw before filling them in on the short version. When Briar finished, Gigi paused her casual perusal and focused as if she was turning the whole thing over in her head, searching for the hidden meaning.

"I never would have expected him to give me the shirt right off his back. He was nice about it, and I can't say I minded the view." Briar took another long sip of her root beer float. "This is pretty awesome stuff, Ann. But I have to ask, where did you find the straws? I didn't think I had any."

Ann leaned back, leveling her with an affronted glare. "Please. I came prepared. Considering you don't pack more than a safety pin as an afterthought in your purse, there was no way I could have expected you to stock your kitchen properly. Now don't change the subject."

"Here! Here! Get back to the hunky boss, turning from suit-wearing asshole to shirtless hero. That sounded promising."

"There's nothing left to discuss. Have you ever considered making this with buttered rum ice cream? I think that could really take this thing up a level…I mean rum. How could it be wrong?"

Ann took the root beer float out of Briar's hand. "Hey! Give that back."

"You have to earn it, missy! We're talking feelings here, and you are clearly in denial about the possibilities." Ann held the drink up over her head, away from Briar.

"What possibilities? I'm sure he'll turn back into a frog tomorrow." Briar rolled her eyes and stood long enough to snatch back her drink before plopping down again. "This isn't a fairy tale. Besides, I'm not in the dating pool. I'm still married."

"The sex possibilities, sweetie." Gigi pulled a low cut teal dress from the closet and held it up to her body, checking herself out in the full-length mirror and posing as she spoke. "When was the last time you got laid?"

Ann tapped the top of Briar's shoulder to get her attention and leaned in, her tone a mock whisper. "Little secret. Sometimes the jerks are the nice ones. They're used to being used, and for a real estate heir like Ciaran Rand, there's money and expectations. If a woman took the time to get past the wall of asshole he built around himself, he's probably one of the good ones."

Briar couldn't help but think of how he offered his shirt on the trail and their mutual understanding of parental expectations and losing a parent. She'd left that part out of the version of events she'd shared. He didn't deserve to have his pain broadcasted for their amusement.

Gigi took up where Ann left off, speaking over her shoulder as she continued to shop Briar's closet. "It's the charmers you have to worry about, and you married a charmer. Do you remember Todd in the beginning? Then later with everyone who wasn't you? That's why I kept pushing you to ditch him in college. It's past time you changed your M.O."

Briar didn't want to admit it, but they made sense. The men she'd been encouraged to date tended to be charmers, but then once she had them, either she got bored, or they did. She only dated them because her mother expected it. That never turned out well. If she'd followed her own heart, she probably never would have married Todd. He happened to be in the right place at the wrong time. Her knee injury put her in a vulnerable place. When he proposed, and her mother got excited, she didn't fight it.

Did Todd cheat on her because he knew that she didn't really love him? Had it been fair to expect fidelity in a loveless marriage? Okay—she wasn't going to absolve him. That would be going too far. She'd been just as trapped, but she managed not to sleep around. Not to mention fucking her mother had been low of not only him but also her mother— unforgivable.

Briar could forgive herself and learn from that mistake. "I don't know myself enough to figure out what I want. All my decisions were weighed against expectation."

Gigi crossed the room, the dress in her hands forgotten as she sat on Briar's other side, sandwiching her in. "Look at the source. No one can blame you for trusting your mother, but after what she did to you, can you really still think that any man she would find good enough is the right kind of man?" Gigi hooked an arm around Brair's shoulders. "You should follow your own desire. Beat your own path, but if you need a guide, we'll be here. Listen to me or better yet—listen to Ann. I didn't and almost missed out on the best man that ever happened to me. She's like the dating whisperer. She used reverse psychology to get me right where I needed to be."

"He pisses me off, and it gets me excited." Heat flooded Briar's cheeks as the admission slipped out. "It's that feeling like I'm about to run a race—the drive to win. When he baits me using my clothes—the one thing I do that has always just been about what I want—it makes me want to push back harder."

Gigi passed her the dress. "So let's do it. Let's plan out some outfits and see just how big of an asshole he is. With enough encouragement, I bet he breaks and seals the deal. This color brings out your eyes."

"Not this one." Briar put one arm around each of her friends, pulling them in for a side hug as the smile started to tug at her lips. "I've got a new lavender dress that makes me feel like a goddess. I guess you get to play Barbie, after all."

Chapter 6

WHO WOULD HAVE THOUGHT THAT HUMP DAY OF all days could usher in an attitude change? Certainly not Briar. Nevertheless, the evidence was sitting beside her on a Chesterfield sofa with his shirt sleeves rolled up and his tie pulled loose. Not sloppy loose, just enough to be on the right side of sexy. Hell, he'd even gotten her coffee right. Apparently, he'd been paying attention, because today there'd been no creamers or sugar to fix it, but the first sip was perfect. Yet another sign there might be more to Ciaran.

If you had asked her yesterday, she might have said this level of charming wasn't possible. She'd taken the advice of her girlfriends and dressed to provoke him. Silly and maybe ridiculously flirty, but she walked a razor-thin line with the rules.

He noticed. She could see it in his eyes. Even if he was

holding his tongue.

She'd already had enough of his silence. "Are you about ready for a break? I know I'm at a good stopping point with the list of items we discussed."

They'd been good little worker bees sticking faithfully to Jack's master schedule—two very long, very quiet hours.

Ciaran lifted his wrist to look at the time. "Yeah, I suppose we could. The day's almost over though. Do you want to put in some extra time and keep grinding on this after our break?"

She'd like to grind something alright. "That shouldn't be a problem." She could be late for her scheduled interrogation by the girls at their favorite watering hole.

He leaned forward, set his laptop on the coffee table, and then stretched his arms over his head before leaning back, arms spread wide along the rear of the sofa. He crossed his feet at the ankle and propped them up beside the forgotten laptop. "You wanted a break. Go ahead. Relax. You aren't going to offend me."

So agreeable today, was this the real Ciaran or was the foot-in-mouth asshole she'd been dealing with the real deal? After last night's too brief chat on the trail, she wanted to know the real answer. She could rile him up and find out. It could be so easy.

"Thanks. You know it is a little hot in here." Briar kept her tone light—very don't look at the man behind the curtain—buying herself some shock value at least she hoped.

Standing or walking through the office for the casual employee she had to deal with; there was nothing wrong with her outfit. For most of the day, she'd even worn a very business appropriate sweater. She kept it buttoned through their morning briefing, and Ciaran hadn't said a thing. She had a scandalous amount of cleavage, but he'd be sending home half the women in this building if he commented on that. Didn't mean she couldn't tempt him.

Briar set her laptop to the side and unbuttoned the sweater. Up to this point all of their interactions had been accident, or without any premeditation. Now she was making a choice there would be no going back from. As she leaned forward and pulled the sleeves down her arms, she revealed the low cut violet neckline of her dress underneath. Ciaran took a sharp breath in but otherwise held back any commentary. She turned her face away to hide her smile as she set the sweater beside her own computer—but she wasn't finished yet.

She leaned back, mirroring him and crossed her legs at the knee, leaving her feet down. This allowed her skirt to ride up her leg. The not so office appropriate slit in the front gapped open, exposing precious extra inches of her thigh that set her face, and no doubt her very on display cleavage, on fire. Both were likely flushed red if she looked in the mirror instead of holding his heated gaze with one of her own.

"Ms. Goodall?" It was a question, but the way his voice grew deep came across more smolder than censure.

"Mr. Rand." This behavior, such a un-Briar-like thing to do—overtly flirt and with someone as inappropriate as her boss.

Should she feel dirty? Maybe. It never seemed to bother Gigi or apparently Ann. If they were right, he might be just what she needed. Neither she nor Ciaran would cross a line, not with their careers at stake. There couldn't be any real harm. The small thrill she got from pushing just this little bit would be enough for her. After spending so much of her life in pursuit of perfect—this, whatever it was that drove her to push him and goad him into a response, tasted like liberation.

That's when it dawned on her—exactly what this behavior was. As children when a boy liked a girl, he wasn't nice, not at first. Boys panicked at the new strange feeling. Little boys told little girls they had cooties. They called the girl names and gave themselves "cootie shots" in the arm. If she was right, Ciaran was little more than a ten-year-old boy in a grown man's body, but instead of passing notes through a friend, he had Jack send calendar meeting invites.

Briar couldn't help the bubble of laughter that snuck out as she visualized the comparison. Her cheeks ached with the muscle strain of keeping her smile suppressed, even if the giggle had gotten loose.

"What's so funny?"

"Just thinking. We've been acting like a couple of kids in grade school at their first dance. I was picturing us at ten-year-olds, playing office in our Sunday best."

His eyebrows went up along with the corners of his mouth in a matching smile. "Why do you say that?"

"Oh come on." She leaned forward, her arms braced on her knees forcing her small breasts together. Bonus points for him—his eyes never left hers. "From the moment we met you've been after me about dress code for every accidental infraction I've made in the last two days. Today I do it on purpose just to see what you'll do and not a word."

"On purpose?"

"Ciaran, a woman doesn't leave the house with a neckline

this low unless she wants someone to notice."

"And why do you want me to notice?"

Briar had been asking herself that same question since the moment she left her borrowed apartment. Really, since her discussion with the girls, it sat simmering in the back of her mind. That question required a lot more honesty than she cared to give him. You didn't exactly tell a man that your ex-husband made you feel like half a woman and that in two days, he'd somehow given that back to her.

A sharp knock on the door saved her. It also reminded her she was in the office and not a living room free to do as she pleased. Maybe her fishbowl office was more of a blessing than she thought.

"Sorry to interrupt guys." Jack marched through the door, still looking down at his tablet—the damn thing was glued to the man's hand. When he looked up, his eyes bounced between them, his eyebrows raising a little higher with each pass. "This is obviously not a good time. I'll come back."

"No, you won't. Out with it now." Ciaran flung out the command before Jack took two steps back to the door.

He grimaced but faced them. "I had a last minute appointment notification show up on your schedule for this evening." Clearing his throat, Jack kept his attention cast down on his tablet.

In the short time, Briar had known him, Jack proved to be the least judgmental person she'd met in the office and easily the most kind. The man didn't seem to have a malicious bone in his body. Yet regardless of what Jack meant by not looking at her as he spoke, her skin crawled with an intense need to cover herself—as if she had done something wrong. Only her pride held her still. By putting her sweater back on, she'd be agreeing that she should be ashamed. Instead, she reached for her laptop to shut it down and subtly tug the hem of her skirt down.

Ciaran's hand covered hers, his fingers warm over hers and rough against her thigh. Her gaze met Ciaran's intense stare, as he spoke low, directly to her—just to her. "This discussion isn't over. Don't move." He looked back at Jack. "Go on. Where am I supposed to be and when?"

"Dinner reservation for two in thirty minutes at Sauce. I'm afraid it's too late to cancel. Ms. Fitch is already on her way. I tried."

"Fuck." Ciaran's hand tightened over hers as his curse echoed the tension radiating through his touch. And that word—from his commanding and otherwise proper lips echoed her desire instead of the curse she supposed he intended. "Call the restaurant and have them add a third seat to the reservation. If I can't avoid it, I'm making sure it stays business. Thanks, Jack."

Dismissed, Jack scurried out the door.

Ciaran's thumb stroked her thigh in tiny circles with unearned familiarity as he kept her hand pinned. Waves of heat rushed through her in time to each gentle stroke. It burned through her reserves of self restraint to keep from pressing her legs together to relieve the pressure building at the end of that path. If only that thumb were a little further north—what magic could that man work with just his hands?

"Come to dinner with me. We'll have a third wheel to deal with, but all things considered, we could probably use a chaperone." The flame of his eyes blazed with intense drive, even if his smile had a slightly rogue tilt to it.

"And after?"

"Let's get through dinner."

Briar swallowed hard and blindly reached over with her free hand, refusing to break eye contact as she patted the spot on the sofa beside her where her phone had last been. Girl's night was going to have to wait—Gigi would understand.

"I'll cancel my plans." She had never worked harder to say four words in her life.

The heat building between them escalated fast and the hormonal cocktail left in its wake had Ciaran feeling drunk despite being stone sober. In his office, he wondered for a moment if she was up to something. Her behavior seemed like such an about face from the day before—more brazen. Her subtle retreat over Jack's interruption convinced him her words and attempt to flirt with him came from a place of genuine interest that he could trust—interest that matched his own even if the timing was off. It appeared as if she forgot for those fleeting moments where she sat and Jack's entrance reminded her.

Over lunch this afternoon, he'd met his brother and found the perfect building to invest in their development plan. He should be focusing on that, not taking his HR Director to dinner. But here they were, side by side in his leather seats, driving to a restaurant under the explainable guise of work.

Ciaran glanced her direction. The sweater made a return

and Briar buttoned it back up, although she did leave one undone at the top, giving him a tantalizing peak at the swell underneath. The hint of skin, either raised in gooseflesh from his air conditioning or from her nerves, made it difficult to concentrate on the road. All he wanted was to watch her. But what made him smile was the unconscious way she chewed her bottom lip as she texted, mussing her red painted lips. The woman was adorably sexy and she had no idea.

They had yet to return to the conversation they'd been having. Understandable while they were still in the office, but now in his car, with no one to hear or interrupt, her retreat was deafening. She may have started the dance but she was leaving the next move squarely in his court to lead or let drop.

"I'm sorry that we'll have a third wheel at dinner. I'd rather it were just us, and that I could take you out properly. At least having her there, no one will ask questions."

Briar turned the full intensity of her silver blue eyes toward him, her head cocked slightly to one side. "You talk as if someone is watching other than Jack. We don't even know what we're doing." She hesitated, chewing her lip again. One of her hands held her phone face down on her lap and the other played with the black beads around her neck. "I'm not imagining this am I? Us? I'm not one of those desperate women you read about. I don't flirt with my boss."

Ciaran reached over, taking the hand in her lap. "I'm out on the limb with you."

It had been the right thing to say because her shoulders slumped in apparent relief, if the soft smile curling the corners of her perfect lips were any kind of guide. Whether she realized it or not, she had the power to ruin him. More so the further they took this thing between them. They seemed to be running into it headlong.

"What are we doing?" Briar leaned forward, eyes wide, open and trusting.

"Whatever it is, I don't want to stop." He turned his attention back to the street, just in time to make the turn into the parking lot.

Ciaran took his hand back from hers to pull the Audi into the first available space and shut it off. He turned to face Briar and give her his full attention, but she was already climbing from the vehicle.

By the time he got out she was two cars down, walking backwards, grinning at him. "Come on, the sooner we meet Ms. Fitch, the sooner we get to after."

He couldn't help but smile back at that. She wasn't running from him, she was racing to whatever came next. With every passing second, each time her teeth bit into her lip, the need to taste her kiss grew. "Briar, wait." She turned, the wind blowing her hair into her face as he approached. "Before we go in…"

Ciaran framed her face with his hands, running his thumbs over the deepening blush in her cheeks. He walked her backwards like that, staring into each other's eyes until her back rested against the partial obscurity of the building. Ten more feet and anyone could have watched them. As they stood, anyone could walk around the corner of the brick building and catch them.

"Is this okay?" his words were hushed, as if he'd scare her away like a frightened deer, something she'd given him no reason to believe. Hell—she'd been the brave one to start this, until now he only antagonized her. Yet here they stood anyway.

In answer, she went up on her toes, brushing her lips against his, too small against his six-foot frame to give it any kind of intensity. It spoke more than words. He bent to meet her, crushing his lips against hers as he pressed her small, soft body into the brick wall. Her dainty hands closed over his, still framing her face. If he moved them, touched her anywhere other than her face, they might never make it inside. It kept him anchored to reality, when nothing else seemed to—especially not the cinnamon candy sweetness of her mouth as she opened to him.

Much as he hated to do it, he pulled back. "I don't want to go in."

"Then why are we? Who is this person?" Briar swiped at his lips with her thumb. "Hold still and let me fix this."

He let her fuss as he worked out an answer. How do you tell the woman that you want, that she's walking into a date setup? He settled on giving her the straight forward truth. "My grandfather has been trying to marry me off. I cancelled this date twice and he reschedules it every time. She's a business associate and no matter how many times I tell him, he doesn't get that I'm not interested."

The dreamy soft smile that played across Briar's kiss swollen lips faltered. "Is this the same woman who you cancelled on Monday?"

"Yes." Briar looked away but Ciaran turned her face back to his, tracing her jawline with the edge of his fingers. "I'm making it clear that I came with you."

Briar stepped to the side, out of the circle of his

arms, her fingers toying with her beads, which seemed to be her nervous habit. "Maybe until we're on firm ground we should keep this to ourselves. It's easy for me to start over somewhere else, but this is your family business. I'm expendable."

He pressed his lips together, holding onto the warm feeling of their kiss from the moment before as he closed the distance she created. "Let's not tear down what we've started before we even build it. From what I can see, you're a lot of things but expendable isn't one of them." He gripped her elbow, gentle but firm, walking her towards the milling group of people around the restaurant entrance. "The only way out is through it."

Expectations. Briar had been up against them her whole life. This was different, knowing she would be the one judged as fit or unfit rather than held to their destructive flame. It gave her a measure of sympathy for the boyfriends she hadn't wanted but more for the ones that didn't measure up—a category she was certain she would find herself in with Ciaran's grandfather even if he wasn't going to say it.

Ciaran didn't have to. The brunette on the other side of the table was all the evidence Briar needed. Monica Fitch smiled with daggers in her eyes. It reminded Briar vaguely of Todd, sending a chill down her spine that cooled her hormones from a rapid boil to a low simmering heat. The only thing keeping it lit at all was Ciaran's hand on her knee under the table. Those questing fingers stroking her thigh could thaw the coldest ice queen with the way they stoked her inner fire.

"My grandfather tells me you're in residential real-estate and run one of the top marketing departments in that niche for your family's company. I'm interested in urban development trends myself." Ciaran's voice was light and friendly, the way he typically addressed business associates—nothing that would lead Monica to believe she was anything more than that.

"Young professionals want to be in the center of everything. People like you and I—they wait longer to start families and move to the suburbs. We're also finding success with empty nesters. That grew our sales of single-family homes as we encourage them to move downtown into condos as their children have children of their own." Monica leaned forward, practically falling out of her low cut cocktail dress with a sex-kitten smile as if she could temp him before she continued. "I'd be happy to discuss it with you over drinks later when we're alone."

If it hadn't already been clear that Briar was an unwelcome interloper in this situation, that would have spelled it out in no uncertain terms. Monica Fitch had clearly been on board with the suggestion that their companies merge in more ways than paper, even if Ciaran wasn't. Someone should send her a memo, arranged unions for business were no longer in vogue.

"That won't work for me, unfortunately. I barely made it to this. Briar is our new HR Director and we were knee deep in an office policy rewrite. My assistant interrupted to let me know my grandfather scheduled this dinner meeting. I didn't want to stand you up a third time but we have more to do." A thin smile stretched across Ciaran's lips.

At least Briar had managed to clear her lipstick from them before he decided to charge in here. She shuddered to think about the state of her own swollen lips. Matte lipstick was a wonderful thing but its power to hang on for dear life had limits.

"You seem awfully young for such an elevated position." Monica smiled with her bared teeth as she finally acknowledged Briar. "You must be fresh out of college."

No way could Briar force a false smile as both Monica and Ciaran seemed to be. Briar didn't have the emotional space left to be that fake. Keeping her tone even would have to be enough as she answered her wannabe rival. "I'm twenty-seven actually and I can assure you I'm more than adequately qualified."

"I'll bet you are." Monica made a dismissive sound that made Briar's spine straighten and Ciaran's hand tighten on her knee.

This is the kind of snake Ciaran's grandfather wanted him to marry? He probably hadn't cared to vet the woman past her family connection. Briar would introduce Ciaran's grandfather to own manipulative mother if Todd hadn't already whisked her off to god knows where. Her mother and Rand Senior might have enjoyed comparing notes. They appeared to have much in common.

It also struck her that this was another shared synchronicity in both her and Ciaran's lives. They kept popping up with increasing frequency. None of them common, but all of them capable of leaving an unseen mark, as permanent at the demons she tattooed to her arm to make hers visible.

The server chose that moment to interrupt. Something unfortunate might have happened if that had carried on much longer. The girl laid out the menus, her high ponytail bobbed as her attention bounced between the three of them. "Will this be separate tickets?"

"No, one." Ciaran's voice was tight.

The server carried on, either oblivious or so used to other people's drama that she simply didn't care. "Can I start you with a drink and an appetizer or are you ready to order."

Briar was in favor of alcohol. "Gin and tonic, please."

"Water for me." Monica's words came out clipped. Seemed someone else was done trying too.

Ciaran gave Briar a long look, as though surprised by her order. And maybe he was, but she could handle it. Admittedly, her cocktail of choice could be an acquired taste, but if there was ever a time for a stiff drink, this situation qualified.

"I'll have what she's having, thank you." He gestured to Briar.

"I'll go put those in while you take a look at the menu."

"Where did we leave off?" The promise of alcohol coming couldn't even make her smile now that they were alone with Monica again. "Oh I remember—our backgrounds. I don't mind sharing since you ask. After finishing top of my class with an MBA focused on Human Resources and Communication, I sat on the board of my father's company before my family sold our share. You could say I grew up in business administration. I trust your background is something similar?"

Monica cleared her throat and shifted uncomfortably in

her seat. "Would you excuse me for a moment? I need to freshen up." Monica slid from her seat, taking her clutch with her. Odds are she wouldn't come back. Ordering water and now the bathroom—dead giveaway.

Closing her eyes, Briar allowed her head to fall back. "If I wasn't here she wouldn't have been so rude."

His body heat soothed Briar's riled spirit as he leaned in, whispering in her ear, as his hand slid ever so slightly higher up her thigh. "Maybe not, but having you here brought out her true colors and made yours shine."

"Ciaran," her voice came out a strained whisper. "There are people all around us." Briar laid her hand over his to stop him from progressing further.

"What do you say I leave an obscene amount of money on the table and we leave?" Ciaran didn't wait for an answer. He slid his billfold out and tossed a couple of bills on the table. She couldn't say how much since her attention remained trained completely on him, and her own racing heart.

In one beat, two at most, he pulled Briar from the chair, across the restaurant and out the door, leaving Monica to her bitterness. The level of exhilaration pumping through her veins, it was like running a race and winning. Knowing she was so far ahead, the competition would never catch her. He released her hand allowing her to run slightly ahead of him, laughing. When she looked back the predatory heat in his smoldering blue gaze made her shudder with an answering fire.

Briar reached the car, and licked her dry lips as she turned to wait.

Ciaran crowded into her space, pressing her against the side of the sedan. "Have I told you how sexy you are when you run?"

His evidence pressed hard against her belly, hijacking her voice and any coherent thought she had past that.

"I watched you that first day, running up the sidewalk. When you walked into my office I was already hard thinking about trying to find you, but there you were." Ciaran ran his thumb over her bottom lip. "You found me. I wanted you right then across my desk."

"Holy shit."

"Give me one reason I shouldn't put you in the back and spread you out on these leather seats so that I can worship my way up those amazing legs." He whispered the words into her neck and finished on a kiss.

Briar moaned, shuddering against him. His touch burned a trail down her side. Then he reached down and pulled her leg up, making her skirt ride up until the cool fall air hit her exposed lace panties. While his hands were busy, his tongue sliding along the column of her neck almost made her forget how very public they were. How was she supposed to think under those circumstances when all she could do was feel—as if she were a raw nerve?

When she found her voice, it came forced between her heaving gasps for air, as if she were running a marathon instead of making out with him. "Someone will see us."

Ciaran nibbled on her ear lobe and her knees went weak. If he hadn't been pressing her against the car, she would have fallen. "Please," she whispered.

"What do you want, Briar," his sexy growl in her ear added to the fog of lust obscuring her judgement.

The rapidly cooling night cleared the haze. "Not here. Not

like this."

He pulled back and she laid her hand on his cheek as their eyes met. His pupils dilated with the answering lust racing through her veins, made his dark eyes appear like black jewels.

"I want you, but not out in the open like this."

He nodded slowly as he took several shaky deep breaths.

"Are you upset with me?" Her voice came out small.

He answered with a soft kiss. "It has to be right for both of us. Why would I be mad?"

Because her ex would have been. She couldn't say that out loud, not to Ciaran, and at least not now. Truthfully, she was a little surprised that he stopped at all. Ann's words played through her mind as they stood there coming down off the rush, holding onto each other as if they were about to drift away on the lowering tide. The assholes really might be the good ones. How did she know so much?

His voice sounded hoarse as it broke through her thoughts. "Let me take you back to your car. We've been moving at break neck speed. I'm sure both of us could benefit from perspective and time to breathe."

She nodded her agreement, not trusting her voice wouldn't break in a sob.

Ciaran ran his finger under her chin, tilting her face up until she looked into his eyes. Already the black receded, making way for the rich navy underneath. "Hey, I meant what I said. We've known each other three days. I'm in no hurry, Speed Racer."

She smiled at his unconventional endearment.

"There, much better." He opened the passenger

door and held it for her. Your smile is beautiful. I want to see more of it."

She lowered herself into the car, already missing his warmth. He leaned down and gave her another soft kiss before he closed her in and came around. Yeah—Dating Whisperer thy name is Ann. She owed both her friends a coffee.

Chapter 7

"HE SIGNED IT." JAY CUT STRAIGHT TO THE CHASE, not waiting for Briar to greet him when she picked up the line. "He didn't contest a damn thing."

After everything, two months of waiting, having to sell most of their shared possessions, and he didn't even fight her for alimony. "Now I feel like a bitch for having his car repossessed. I assume they haven't found him yet if he was that agreeable." She spun in her chair doing a tiny celebratory dance in her seat for ten seconds before pulling herself together. "Does that mean I'm free? It's really done?"

"I'm on my way down to file it with the clerk of court as we speak. He had the damn thing notarized. You didn't have children and the house was sold to clear debt. Yes. It's done."

Relief pushed through her faster than the lust from last

night. "Thank you, so much, Jay. You've made my day. How soon can I file my name change?"

"I already have the papers drawn up. Just say the word."

"Word." It came out as more of a triumphant squeal, but judging from the laughter on the other end of the line, Jay got the point before he disconnected.

Briar hugged her now silent phone to her chest. Even though he hung up, it was the closest she could get to hug her lawyer. Maybe she should have a funeral for Mrs. Briar Goodall. She'd have to consult the handbook they were currently rewriting regarding changing her name to Sullivan, which would also mean telling Ciaran—an idea that took her joy level down a couple notches.

A knock sounded on the glass, as she set the phone face down on her desk. The man himself walked into her office. Ciaran shut the door and closed her blinds. She wanted to roll her eyes, and just barely suppressed the cynical need to tell him just how *not* suspicious that move was.

His smile was so damn sexy, it gave her strength to keep the sarcasm as bay. "You look awfully happy? Does that smile have anything to do with me?"

"Some of it might." She pursed her lips, biting the inside of her cheek to tone it down.

"I'll take what I can get." He moved behind her, and swept her hair from her neck.

"Is there something I can do for you, Mr. Rand? Before someone walks into my not very private office." There is was; the pessimist in her could only be denied for so long.

"There's my girl." His hands kneaded the muscles of her neck. It felt like heaven. "Must we be so formal?"

She was his girl. He said it. It might scare her if it didn't feel so good to hear the words come from his mouth. A lazy smile spread as his hands worked their magic to relax her.

"We're at work, so yes." Her tone might have been chastising but considering how rapidly she turned to putty under his touch, it lacked conviction.

He tilted her head to the side, and his soft lips and unshaved scruff—which she found turned her on more than the polished version—met the sensitive column of her throat. "I think you may need to stay late today so that we can discuss today's wardrobe choice. You are definitely out of dress code." His voice vibrated along her skin.

"Would there be food involved in this meeting?" Her voice sounded breathy and far away, carried off by the need he was already stoking to life inside her.

"Chinese can be arranged." His hands ran up under her blazer and she felt his smile followed by another kiss. "Strapless, Briar? This is practically lingerie."

"Not practically."

He groaned and stepped back. "I'll have Jack send the meeting invite." He walked around to the right side of the desk putting much needed distance between them. "Patience, Speed Racer. Five o'clock will be here before too long."

She glanced down to see that he was right and smiled as he walked back out of her office with a lopsided smile that matched her own.

Chapter 8

SHE'S EVERYTHING CIARAN NEVER KNEW HE WANTED in a woman—just as she was. Smart and sassy, brazen as hell, but still soft. The thing that surprised him the most was how vulnerable she seemed. It took her from a fantasy that he might never have wasted his time on, to real lover. She made him feel things and forget his priorities until she became one. While he always agreed with his father's choices, he had never been able to see himself making the same.

Now he sat here thinking about a future past this business. All because Briar made her intentions clear and then asked him to wait. Their lives ran such an odd parallel that whether they took it fast or slow, he was certain he couldn't go wrong with her. After last night's abrupt stop, he assumed it would take weeks or at least several dates before they might pick up where they left off, but when she walked in for morning coffee in that skirt and a bustier under her more office appropriate blazer he knew. Her whole outfit was like waiving a red cape at a bull.

"Knock, knock." Briar slipped through the door and closed it behind her.

Ciaran sat in the dark, watching the light through blinds behind him play across her skin, drawing lines across all the places he planned to kiss.

Radiance seemed to roll off her skin in the softer light of early evening. Her need to challenge him, her competitive spirit called out to him. It burned every damn time he had to pull her in his office. Alone, to discuss another dress code rule. Only this time he was going to break the rules and bend her over the desk. Right after he worshiped those legs.

Ciaran watched her saunter around the edge of the desk. He rolled his chair back to give her room for whatever she wanted. More than he needed to have her, he wanted her to be comfortable, to be okay with this. Briar could have the reigns until she was ready to hand them over.

She used the space to perch on the edge in front of him, crossing her legs at the knee so that her too short skirt rode up, exposing that her fishnets ended in a lace band at the top of her very bare thighs. A soft smile played on her lips as she twirled the black beads at her throat. Since his earlier stop in her office, she'd pulled her hair into a high ponytail revealing purple streaks in her hair that he somehow missed yesterday. Or maybe they had always been there. He'd never actually seen her hair up off her neck.

Ciaran couldn't help but smile at that very small but important detail. "Briar, you know party colors are against the rules. I'm afraid you'll have to do something about your hair."

"I think maybe we can come to some kind of arrangement so that I can keep it. Maybe a little quid pro quo." Her voice was light as she leaned forward. The swell of her breasts strained against the fabric of her top.

Ciaran rolled his chair forward, and took her calf between his palms. He stroked the silky grid of lines, up the curve. He uncrossed her legs, letting the one he held rest on the desk. "I've been having full on fantasies about these legs for days."

He repeated his actions with her other leg, stroking the curve. This time he raised her leg to rest on his shoulder. His hands continued stroking up the insides. He turned his head to graze his lips along the inside of her thigh.

"Ciaran," her voice was husky and her silver gray eyes flashed with something that made him wonder if he already pushed too far.

He didn't want to stop, but he'd meant what he told her the night before. He would stop no matter what if she needed it. "Tell me what you need."

Briar's lips curled into a wicked smile that sent relief and lust on a race, burning inside him. "Hurry up, there's something I've been meaning to try."

He grabbed her ass and pulled her forward, forcing her to fall back on her elbows so that she could still watch him. Her legs spread wider to accommodate him. "You're right. I can take my time later."

Briar bit back the tiny shriek from his sudden move as she slid forward on the desk. He had her spread wide; her skirt rucked up to her waist, exposing the black lace thong she put on for him when she dressed that morning. She hated the damn thing, but if she were going to ruin her panties in the rush to have sex, she did what any good girl would so she didn't wreck her favorites. These she didn't mind sacrificing to the cause.

His eyes moved across the full display, clearly hungry to touch and play, but other than pull her closer, he hadn't made a move. "You are the hottest, damn thing I've ever touched." He traced a finger up the top of her thigh.

"Are you going to keep talking or prove it?" She shouldn't goad him, but he'd been so nice. She wanted a little more of the asshole that made her hot. She could appreciate basking in the glow of this side. She fully intended to. He could make love to her later. Right now, she wanted him to fuck her.

Ciaran's nostrils flared and then he lowered his mouth to her sex, sucking her clit through the lace. Briar's head lolled back as immediate pleasure rocked through her—nearly enough to make her scream as her hips bucked up. He hooked a finger at the edge of her panties and pulled them down her legs.

"Was that fast enough for you, baby." His voice was deep with the needs he ignored for himself to meet her pleasure first.

She giggled, and then forced a sober expression as he pressed first one and then two fingers inside her aching channel.

It tore an involuntary moan from her lips. The throb built inside of her like a second heartbeat in answer to his rhythm. She'd been so worked up waiting that she might go off like a rocket for him with almost no effort. Each stroke, sawing in and out of her and every circle around her clit with his thumb drove her higher.

Briar couldn't hold herself up to watch him work anymore. Couldn't hold his gaze, staring into the ocean of his eyes as she fell headlong into something better than she had with anyone or anything not battery operated since—ever. When his tongue replaced his thumb on her clit, her back arched up off his desk, making her breasts spill from her top. She pushed the satin bustier down and palmed her own breasts.

His muffled moan told her he was still watching. She pulled at her nipples, sending a spark of pain to mix with her pleasure. It was exactly what she needed to go over the edge. She released her breast to cover her mouth and stifle the scream that clawed at her throat as her body became the pulse inside of her, rolling in pleasure on wider and wider waves until they slowed and stilled. Through the whole thing he didn't stop. He waited for her to take her fill—completely unselfish.

Briar groaned as her limbs went limp. "Please tell me you've got a condom because I want you inside of me.

He loomed over her, trailing kisses up her stomach as he pushed the satin up from the bottom. "Can you even move?"

Instead of answering immediately, Briar rolled to her stomach under him, forcing Ciaran to back up as she slid down the desk until her heels touched the floor. She shucked her blazer—the only office appropriate item in her outfit—to the floor. The tail of her ponytail tickled her shoulder as she looked back at him. "Unhook my top."

Ciaran did as ordered with efficiency, letting it drop to the floor, so that his hands could take over the task of rolling her nipples. Having a man be this greedy to touch her, this could become an addiction. Right now, she wanted something else.

She held his hands still with her own. "Condom, Ciaran."

Ciaran, pulled one hand out from under hers, moving it lower, but keeping it in contact with her until he reached her sex. He released her other breast to glide his hand up her back, pushing her down so the she bent forward. Briar's sensitized nipples pressed flat against the wood, still warm from her body heat.

Then she felt him. One hand gripped her hip; fingers splayed and pressed into her soft flesh. The other moved the head of his cock up and down her folds, sending languid pleasure through her post orgasmic bliss. It rekindled the ripples of pleasure that had just subsided. Fuck—this was going to be amazing.

"Is this what you want, every time you tease me?" He gripped her ponytail, tugging it gently to turn her face toward him. "Do you want it?"

"Yes." Her skin tingled, nerves making her muscles tremble with the strain of holding herself together. Briar pressed back against him, impaling herself on him. Not enough. Just the beginning of him. "Take me," she demanded.

He drove himself to the hilt, filling her nearly to the brink of her tolerance. A soft shriek broke free from her lips. He leaned forward, using her ponytail to guide her mouth to his. It lifted the top of her body to a more comfortable angle. He wrapped his arm around the front of her, holding her smashed into him as they kissed. She writhed beneath him as he ground into her.

Neither of them could keep this pace. A punishing grind that fired off the orgasm that never really left her. This one a more powerful climax than the first with the delicious resistance of his hard length pumping in and out of her and her body fighting to hold him in. He swallowed her screams of pleasure with his lips. His body shook behind her as he groaned into their shared kiss. He held still, pressing her body flat into his.

He released her, letting her stumble forward as he dropped back into his chair.

"Fuck, I'm sorry. I didn't mean to be so rough. You deserve better." He held out his arms to her, waiting for her to climb in his lap. She blinked back at him, frozen in place. Why was he apologizing for great sex? The fact that he wanted to cuddle made her want to reward him in much more entertaining ways, after they regained some stamina over takeout.

"Ms. Goodall, I owe you an apology, so get your ass over here so I can deliver." The reminder of her married name brought with it an unwelcome stab of guilt that nibbled at the raw edges of her glow. She needed to tell him. She should have told him already. But not now. After the famine of affection she'd only just escaped, she couldn't chance the premature loss of the feast she found herself in now. Her secrets needed to remain in the dark—at least for tonight.

Ciaran waited for her with open arms as her post-coital high started to slip at that far off look in her eyes. Briar smiled and the knot that formed in his stomach at the idea of having hurt her dissipated.

She pulled him from the chair by his hand, and led him to the sofa. Considering his pants were around his ankles, he was less then graceful, but he managed to step free of them, and deposit the condom in the trash on the way. She pushed him back and picked up the laptop he'd left on the coffee table earlier in the day before she settled back in the crook of his arm.

"I've been distracting you since yesterday afternoon. Think you can write policy while naked and eating Chinese?" Briar asked.

Ciaran looked down at her. She was already lost in thought pulling up the documents she needed.

Had he missed something? Women loved to cuddle and talk feelings. On the rare occasion he took the time to have a girlfriend, both those tasks were immediately on the agenda. As far as he was concerned, if he was spending time naked with her, risking his career and ultimate goal to be with her, this was a damned relationship.

Ciaran pulled the device from her hands and leaned forward to set it back on the table. "This isn't work time. You clocked out at five when you walked through my door."

Briar turned, to face him so that she draped across his lap, her back to the empty room. Blinking up at him, she traced her finger along each of his shirt buttons until she reached the few at the bottom he bothered to open. "How did we miss most of your shirt?"

He raised and dropped his shoulders to shrug. "I seem to recall someone demanding I pick up the pace."

"Well, I had to wait a whole other day after getting so worked up last night." A teasing smile played softly on her lips, making him feel the first flush of his returning stamina. "I meant I didn't want it in the parking lot, not that I didn't want it at all."

She ran her finger lightly up his spent cock. Taking it in her hand, she stroked slowly, watching it come back to life. She slid from his lap to kneel on the floor between his spread knees. The daylight was almost completely gone now and Ciaran had no strength to resist her in his state of semi-arousal and no desire to find a light switch to break the spell she was weaving around them.

"What are you doing?" His voice came out harsh in the quiet, but she smiled anyway.

"Making up for lost time. I said there was something I wanted to try."

Ciaran wanted to talk. They would have plenty of time to fuck, but with each downward stroke, he lost sight of the reason. He couldn't see past the need to be inside her again, any way she wanted him.

"Honey, where are the condoms?" Those doe eyes and her sugar sweet way of asking held him captive. "We can talk if you want to or we can enjoy each other. If you're worried about my motivation, I promise I'm after more than your body. It's just been a while."

How was he supposed to tell her no when she looked at him that way? "Top drawer."

She crawled the short distance, giving him a view that had him more than ready when she returned with the box and a wide smile. "Layback, I'll take over for a while." She pulled out a strip of three. "You should save your strength."

Chapter 9

"YOU BITCH. I GAVE YOU THE DAMN DIVORCE YOU wanted. Why'd they take my car?"

Briar winced as she sat back in her white leather chair. Crossing her legs at the knee, the fabric of her jeans dug into tender places. "Hello, Todd. How can I help you today?"

"You had them repossess my car. What the fuck do you think you're playing at?" His angry voice crackled across the line.

She sighed loud enough for him to hear as she spun slowly in her seat. Hindsight, calling the bank on the car had been a low blow. Todd wasn't wrong that he gave her everything she wanted—in the light of morning the whole vile thing had turned out better for her in the end.

Still Briar didn't feel sorry for him.

Her voice dripped artificially sweet with her bitterness. "When you don't make your payments, those kinds of things happen."

"Why didn't you make my payments?"

She rolled her eyes at his entitled tone, but the spoiled child she had been married to couldn't hear an eye roll so she elaborated. "I stopped paying when I opened the bedroom door. Ask your new piece of ass. Oh—wait, she dissolved her company and went bankrupt. You didn't know that, did you? Did you actually think that you traded up?"

It was the whole reason Briar came home early that day.

"Get it back," his voice snapped like a whip.

Old Briar would have jumped at the command, ready to be the obedient wife. The well-sated version he called today had a better agenda just down the hall. "I fail to see how that's my problem. Have a nice day."

She swiped at the phone and left it face down on her desk. She leaned back in the chair and closed her eyes as she toyed with the frayed edge of her fashionably distressed jeans. She counted to twelve before her phone started to vibrate across the surface of her desk.

"Are you going to answer that?" the low rumble of Ciaran's voice rolled through her, like Tom Hiddleston reading math, but without the yummy British accent.

His voice left a smile tugging at the corners of her lips. She laid her hand over the device, holding it still until it stopped. "Not particularly. The only person I want to talk to is standing in my office."

It earned her a half smile, as if he was trying not to but couldn't seem to help himself. These were the truly sexy ones that made her forget her surroundings, at least until her phone buzzed again, dancing across the surface of her desk. "Now you want to talk." Ciaran shook his head. "You're just trying to avoid the lecture on dress code you know is coming. Those jeans, Ms. Goodall."

Just that easily he killed the smile he'd given her. She looked down at her distressed denim rather than met his eye. They didn't jive with the policy they'd finally written together, but that was exactly why she wore them.

"What? It's Friday."

For her efforts at mock innocence, he rewarded her with a smile. "My office in five minutes. I got us some coffee to make up for what you missed this morning and you can tell me how the trip to the lawyer went."

Fuck.

Briar picked at another spot on her jeans. Could she distract him with sex? Did she want to in the middle of the day when anyone could catch them? Probably not, and hell no. That meant she had to say it. She was divorced. He'd see the name when the social security card came back anyway. Did she think she could hide it forever? He would find out as soon as he meet Gigi if Ann didn't get to him first. Both would threaten him within an inch of his life and not hesitate to tell him why.

She crossed her fingers that coffee included more than just her.

Five minutes waiting for her was long enough to make his day go to shit. His brother Hamish wouldn't wait. There was another investor checking out the building and he needed to put in the bid. Ciaran dreaded asking Rand Senior for anything. However, it didn't outweigh his need to finish this business deal and bring his family back together.

If Rand Senior said no, he had a decision to make and a non-compete clause. He could afford this investment himself. He had the money to buy in on his own. As a single man with a salary larger than he needed, he'd saved and invested it. He meant the nest egg for when someone like Briar came along. Of course, in his plans that was still years out, but she raced into his life now, and he needed to be clear on where this relationship would lead—and what he wanted.

If Briar wasn't on the same page, Ciaran would let the deal pass and continue as they were until she caught up. The only part in any of this that felt right was her. He wasn't sure when that changed. Probably somewhere over dinner with Monica Fitch. But that might only have been the push he needed to see it, rather than the moment. Actually having to sit across from the future his grandfather wanted for him, while sitting beside the warm and vibrant woman who in four days made him want to charter a plane for Vegas, had drastically shifted the lens through which he viewed his life.

The sense that something had altered her attitude followed her into his office as she entered. The smile she'd given him so casually in her office had been replaced by her teeth digging into her bottom lip. Four days hadn't given him the wisdom to know if that always meant something bad. The pinched look between her eyes and the way she couldn't seem to look up past the tips of her own shoes filled in the blanks for him.

She pushed up the sleeves of her oversized white sweater and instead of the beads that she always seemed to toy with she fiddled with the large black watch that looked out of place on her dainty arm. She picked up her coffee as she sat leaving space between them.

"What's going on up there?" He gently gripped her arm and pulled her forward to lay a chaste kiss on her forehead, before letting her relax back into the distance she seemed to crave. For the first time it occurred to him that, he might have hurt her last night and she hadn't told him. She was an athletic woman but the difference in size might have mattered. More so if she hadn't had those sky high heels on. The standing sex might not have worked without them. He pushed the thought from his mind before his dick had a chance to react. "I didn't do anything wrong, did I?"

Briar laid her head on his shoulder. "You were amazing. I just need to tell you something that I'm pretty sure you won't like."

Ciaran leaned back slightly to watch the pensive look on her face. How bad could this get? They rushed into this, so there was bound to be things he didn't know. They would get through it. They got out of their own damn way, hadn't they? Hell, they had turned their need to pick at each other into foreplay at this point.

"Say it. You'll feel better and then we can get past it."

She took a deep breath, clearly bracing herself. "Yesterday when you asked why I was so happy, it wasn't about you. It was something I had to clear up back in St. Cloud. It had to do with the phone call I didn't want to answer when you were in my office."

He recalled the conversation. He'd been totally absorbed in their banter both times. Taking a drink of his coffee, he hoped the bitterness would alleviate his sudden dry mouth as he waited for her to finish.

She sketched lazy circles on the thigh of his 501s as she continued, "My ex-husband signed the divorce papers yesterday." She scrunched up her face and let her head fall forward so that her hair obscured her face, letting the purple streaks she added peek out. "I went to the lawyer to sign documents that will change my name back to Sullivan. I'm Briar Sullivan, not Briar Goodall."

Ciaran let out the breath he had been holding and pressed his palm to his chest. His mind raced back to her sudden attitude change after they slept together; he thought he was being cute calling her Ms. Goodall. The relief burst into laughter.

Briar scrambled sideways before moving to stand, but he pulled her back down. "Wait, let me explain." He wrapped his arms around her waist to hold her until he had her attention.

Briar crossed her arms over her breasts, voice wavered with emotion. "I'm serious and you're laughing. I've got no idea what the hell I'm even doing."

His reaction probably made him look deranged, but all he wanted was to kiss her and maybe try that reverse cowgirl on the Chesterfield again.

When she sat still, he loosened his hold. "I never told you why I'm supposed to inherit the company even though my father is still living and I have an older brother."

"What do they have to do with anything?" Briar's eyes

were shining with unshed tears. She still, clearly assumed the death of their unconventional romance was imminent instead of acknowledging the firm ground it took root in without her noticing.

"Jamison Rand Senior, my grandfather, cut off his only son because he married a pregnant divorcee, my mother. Other than you not being pregnant…" Ciaran paused and lifted her chin to look directly at him. "You aren't, right?"

She shook her head. Her eyes were wide, and her mouth hung open in surprise.

Ciaran pulled her closer, leaning his forehead against hers. "If we fly to Vegas tonight, and I'm not saying we are, I will have completed the circle and become my father. I couldn't be happier." No reason for her to know he really had been thinking about Vegas and her in the same sentence all morning.

Sparkling with tears, her gray eyes held onto them like her face would melt. Instead of letting them go, she traced her fingers along the beginnings of his beard growth. She pulled him into a brief kiss, interrupted by a clamber at the door. Again, she tried to leap from his lap, but now the consequences didn't matter and he wasn't letting her move.

Jack's voice carried through the opening door. "Mr. Rand, your grandson is in the middle of a meeting. If you'll just wait. I'll let him know you're here."

"Let him in, Jack."

His friend and longtime assistant turned with a horrified expression, his eyes wide as Jamison Senior shoved the larger man out of the way. He was yelling before he even noticed the compromising position they were in.

"Young man, do you know the trouble I went to in order

to get you that date with Monica Fitch? You finally go after three cancelations and I have to hear in the country club that you were playing footsy at the table with some escort and making out in the damn parking lot. I thought I raised you better!" By the time he finish, his haggard voice wheezed.

Ciaran's spine straightened but he drew strength from the woman sitting calmly on his lap. For all her panic, now that the crisis found them out, she held herself perfectly still. Only moving to slip her slim hand in his.

A vain pulsed at the old man's temple as he pounded his cane on the floor. "Is this the floozy now? You brought your kept woman to my office?"

Jack made a choking sound behind Rand Senior.

Ciaran narrowed his eyes at the old man as Briar slid slowly off his lap.

"She is neither a kept woman nor a floozy. My mother taught me better manners than to speak that way about a woman, especially in the lady's presence." Ciaran stood and Briar moved to stand at his side, fingers still twined with his. His voice remained calm, lacking both the vitriol and malice of his mentor. "And since this is the first time you've set foot in the building in more than one year, this is my office. You are only a figurehead. I run this business now and I'd like to see you run it without me."

Briar extended her right hand to Jamison Senior, attempting the softer voice of reason. "I'm your HR Director, Briar Sullivan." He glared at the appendage as though it were covered in gore. She let her hand drop back to her side.

The old man stammered as his face turned a deeper shade of red, his eyes bulged as the thinned lips in his cragged face turned white with his increased rage. "All the years I wasted on you, boy. Only to have you turn your position into a mockery!"

Ciaran had enough. He focused his full attention on Briar. "Speed Racer, honey, how do you feel about industrial loft homes? I'm switching family businesses. Seems there are some exciting development opportunities. Ground floor on what appears to be an up-and-coming industry."

She pressed her lips together in a tiny smile, whether from the job offer or the endearments he couldn't be sure, but then she leaned into him squeezing his hand tight.

"Did I ever tell you my parents were in the salvage business before I helped Mother liquidate? I'd be happy to lend my experience. I formally resign my position as HR Director for Rand Enterprises." She squared her shoulders and held her hand out for Ciaran to take it, as though they were meeting for the first time instead of being new lovers. "I've been offered a position with a rising development company. It's too good to pass up."

Ciaran used the handshake to pull Briar in until her body flattened against his. He closed the deal with a kiss, not as heated as it might have been if they were alone, but enough that Jack cleared his throat to remind them where they were. The audience didn't matter. Jamison Senior should see exactly the loyalty he lost.

When he pulled back, she closed her eyes and a soft smile lit up her face. "Thank god, I'm not the only one of us in love."

"I fell way before you did." He dipped her like the heroine in a movie. "But I'm afraid I have to insist on business casual at the office."

Her laughter was immediate, "Only if I can break the rules."

"Baby, that's the whole reason we'll have them."

Epilogue

BRIAR HEARD THAT SOME PEOPLE—APPARENTLY GIGI was one of them—didn't find tattoos to be painful after the first few minutes. Yes, Briar found the experience cathartic—a way to express a part of herself that she couldn't put into words—but every second hurt. After five hours in the chair, she struggled not to squirm under the fire raging from the new ink under her skin. This called for a distraction ASAP. The novel she brought along failed at this task miserably but something had to do the trick. Her new art cost too much to spoil.

Random thoughts flashed at her through the pain like a dealer with a deck of cards until one stuck out. Monday morning—perhaps she'd wear a sleeveless dress to work. Just thinking about strutting into Ciaran's new office—waiting to be called out—had a smile tugging at the corners of her mouth. Of course, he would know about the tattoo before then, since she spent most nights at his loft. But the idea of being spread across his desk Monday after a little policy foreplay took her mind off the half sleeve currently being etched into her skin.

"What's so funny?" Declan lifted the needle from her arm and stared at her with one eyebrow raised. "Most people don't think this tickles."

Briar did laugh out loud at his deadpan attempt at humor. This man had something going for him, even if Ann wouldn't admit to it. "Just thinking about breaking dress code to show off my ink."

"Oh! Can I help you pick out your outfit?" Gigi breezed in from the gallery side, hands clapped together in mock prayer. "You know I love helping you be bad. I can call Ann and make it a girls' day. We'll just start at your place."

Declan turned away at the mention of Ann and concentrated on smoothing balm over Briar's fresh ink. Poor dude had the brooding leading man act down. Too bad his leading lady wasn't interested—at least that's what she claimed. Between the bathroom conversation months ago and Ann's obvious avoidance, Briar wanted to call bullshit. Maybe a girls' day would be the perfect opportunity to do a little recon and find out if Ann was serious about her office booty call. If something could be salvaged that might make her friends happy, it would be worth it. Both Ann and Declan were part of their little tribe, even if Briar didn't know him well. She wanted all her friends to have the kind of happiness she found with Ciaran.

The door chimed to signal a new arrival. Gigi turned to head up front, but Briar reached out and grabbed her hand. "I think I can make tomorrow work. If not, we'll do next weekend for sure."

Gigi grinned and squeezed Briar's hand in answer before heading up front. The buzz of Declan's tattoo gun hummed to life again for the finishing touches—wishful thinking before she went back to work on distracting her mind.

Girl time would be good for all of them. Briar learned a few things since dissolving her marriage. First, to put energy into those who stood by you without judging—and that meant Ann and Gigi. Her love life may be on track now, but they were by her side while she was a hot mess. Second, not to lose herself. With Ciaran, the second lesson proved easy to follow. Now that she found someone who didn't ask her to change—who valued her and didn't treat her as an object or commodity—it made her wonder everyday how she managed to stay in a loveless marriage for so long.

"Plan for next weekend." Speak of the devil—Ciaran leaned against the half wall that divided Declan's booth from the others. "I heard you girls chatting when I came in. I've got plans for you, but I can make myself scarce next weekend while you have fun."

Ciaran clearly dressed for a day out. A view Briar appreciated, even if she did feel shabby by comparison in her yoga pants and a tank top chosen out of healthy respect for a day filled with pain,. Two months warming Ciaran's bed did nothing to cool the instant lust that towed her under when he entered a room. This man made a dress shirt, jeans, and a sport coat sexy. On anyone else, the ensemble might have made him look like a yuppie, but with that five o'clock shadow and cocksure grin, he got away with it.

The buzz of the tattoo gun went silent again and Briar

realized she hadn't felt a thing as she'd been watching Ciaran. The perfect diversion. She'd have to remember that for future ink.

"All done. Go have a look in the mirror." Declan rolled back his stool from the old-fashioned Barber chair to give her space. "When you're done, I'll bandage you up and get you on your way."

Briar eased out of the chair, her flip flops clopping on the hardwood floor as she crossed the room to the mirror. Ciaran's following gaze burned like another tattoo without any of the pain, branding her as his. She couldn't look any less sexy today, but for Ciaran that didn't seem to be an issue. After her disaster of a first marriage, the idea of belonging to someone should have scared her. With Ciaran, it didn't. She had the sense that he would belong to her, as well. Equals. What marriage should be. If anything, she valued this mutual belonging more because she knew the flip side.

Standing sideways, Briar admired the black and gray masterpiece wrapped around her shoulder and upper arm to her elbow. Shadow and light brought to life the archangel, wings spread behind him, sword raised in battle with a demon trampled under his feet. Declan captured the Italian Renaissance painting perfectly. She never should have worried about asking for such a specific piece—*St. Michael Overwhelming the Demon* by Raffaello Sanzio. Even with the slight alteration to make it fit her arm, he nailed it.

Her mother and ex hated tattoos. So her first sleeve of demons symbolized the negative people and events in her life holding her back. Maybe it had been a stupid reaction to divorce, but at the time it felt right, and she didn't regret it. This new tattoo represented her triumph over those forces in her life. This life reflected her. Not someone else's imposed ideal.

The warmth of Ciaran moving up behind her, had her body tingling, reacting as if he sent out some signal only she could feel even before he wrapped his arm around her midriff and kissed the exposed side of her neck. His dark stare met her gray one in their reflection. "It suits you, Speed Racer."

"Yes, it does." Briar snuggled back into his embrace, as she continued to admire her new art.

"It'll look great in our wedding photos in Vegas."

Briar craned her head back to look up at him. "Was that a proposal?"

"Would you say yes if it was? I mean, if you have better plans for the weekend…" he let the question hang.

She scrutinized his features. His hold on her remained relaxed and his tone easy, but the tension around his eyes and in the set of his jaw gave him away. Hell—even the way he asked showed that he was braced for her refusal. This came too soon—at least it should have been. Somehow it didn't feel that way. This time would be different. It already was.

Briar went up on her toes, twisting enough to brush her lips against Ciaran's before answering in a hushed voice, "Let's go pack."

The smile that spread across his face silenced Briar's last whispers of doubt—which sounded suspicious like her mother anyway. His grip around her middle tightened and he spun her as he laughed. When her feet touched the ground again, Briar turned in his embrace to face him. Circling her arms around his neck, Ciaran met her halfway. His lips crashed into hers with bruising force. His joy matching her own so strongly that it might as well have been a living thing.

When Ciaran pulled back, his expression turned sober—at least he tried, but failed miserably at the attempt. "Can we get married by an Elvis impersonator? I'm having fun imagining the fit my grandfather will have when we send him a picture."

The image that sprung to mind sent her into a fit of giggles. With her first-hand reference from the day Rand Senior discovered them in Ciaran's office, the image was pretty vivid. "I think we have to. What are the odds we can get through the experience without a wardrobe malfunction?"

"It wouldn't be us if we did."

This begged the question—what should a bride wear to a Vegas wedding? Now that Briar found the love of her life, she had a dress code to break.

The list of songs that shaped my words for Briar and Ciaran evolved over the course of writing this book, but they were always on auto repeat until I finally typed out "the end". Enjoy the mood music.

Perfect – Alanis Morisette

Thunder – Imagine Dragons

That I Would Be Good – Alanis Morisette

Inner Demons – Julia Brennan

Rise Up – Imagine Dragons

Whatever You Want – Pink

Wicked Game – Cover performed by Theory of a Deadman

Break the Cycle – You+Me

You & I – John Legend

She Sets the City On Fire – Gavin DeGraw

Love Exists – Amy Lee

I Am Here – Pink

Check out the first book in the Ink & Brazen women series…

Sneak Peak

Skin deep

She's looking for Mr. Right Now.
He's planning on forever.

Gigi Duval doesn't do relationships, especially with her hear and career on the line. She values two things—her image and a good time in the bedroom. Watching men lie and cheat her whole life hardened her against "happily ever after." When she interviews with Roman Bishop, the sexy co-owner of Ink Spinners Tattoo, she begins to wonder if he might be more than just a casual fling. Only one thing is certain: Roman is off limits. Gigi can't possibly add her best friend's brother to her trusty little pink book. Or can she?

Turn the page for a sneak peek.

chapter 1

*t*here were few things more uncomfortable than the morning after—awkward text messages, ignored phone calls, or the not so random meeting in the street. As Gigi Duval deleted yet another dick pic off her phone, she decided last night's fuckboy was testing every one.

She took another sip of her latte and then forced a sociable smile on her perfectly glossed lips. She'd met her best friend, Ann Kennedy, for coffee at their favorite café in the rehabbed NewBo neighborhood. She loved the brick building with its original tin ceiling, high gloss wood tables and metal bistro chairs. It smelled like freshly brewed coffee and soul.

"Which play date is harassing you now?" Ann asked with a knowing smirk, one expertly drawn blonde eyebrow raised.

They were meeting over Ann's lunch break, so she dressed accordingly in a navy silk top and khaki cropped dress slacks. Her severe, flat-ironed hair and neutral makeup choices were selected with a strategic eye to reflect her poised businesswoman image.

Gigi turned the phone face down as it dinged yet again. She tapped her pink polished nails on the floral plastic case in annoyance. "One whose name will be erased from my little pink book when I get home."

"Sounds like you didn't enjoy your walk of shame."

Some variation of this conversation started most of Gigi's lunch dates with her best friend. You would think Gigi called a new date every night. Her lips curved up into a smile as her shoulders raised in a non-committal shrug. "Don't be ridiculous—I prefer the term slut strut."

"I can't wait for someone to catch your eye for more than a quick fling," Ann sighed as she pushed a piece of salad across her plate. "You can't keep this up forever. It's not safe."

Gigi shrugged, brushing off her concern. Men caught her eye on a regular basis. The problem was choosing one. Years ago, she learned men could have as many women as they wanted and no one seemed to care. So why couldn't she have the same? Who made the rule that she couldn't have no-strings-sex and save her heart from one brutal let down after another?

Did she ever get tired of it? Absolutely. She was

tempted to retire the little pink book all the time. Just last night for example. She sat waiting for Dick Pic—a colossal waste of time—when a tattooed god-among-men had approached her and offered to buy her a drink. *You're too classy for a dive like this, beautiful.* He hadn't been rude or handsy. He just sat there chatting with her, keeping her company and the lechers away until her date arrived—a full thirty minutes late—and then drifted back to his friends.

"What are you up to today besides mischief?" Ann asked.

Gigi released the breath she had been holding at Ann's sudden change in topic. "Just chasing job leads and then dinner with the parents. Nothing too exciting."

"Speaking of family connections, would you like a new lead?" Ann reached into her Kate Spade bag and pulled out her tablet, an iPad Pro that Gigi had been salivating over for months. "My step-brother just opened a tattoo shop and needs someone to be his office manager. Just basic stuff, run the front desk, setup and run his website. Nothing you haven't done before."

Grabbing a business card out of the tablet's case, she slid it across the table. Gigi picked it up, running her fingertips over the embossed skull design.

A tattoo shop wasn't exactly the kind of place she would have applied. She also hadn't planned on leaving the bank, but her former employer cornered her in his office for a little quid pro quo. She gave her immediate notice to the HR department. The ink wasn't even dry on her resignation before she was out the door. Now it had been a month and her savings would only hold out so much longer. At the very least, this could tide her over while she found something else.

"I'll pop down there and give him my resume." Gigi slipped the card into her purse and picked up her latte for another sip. "But I'm keeping my options open."

Ann rolled her eyes as she put her tablet away. "Just do me a favor and keep his name out of your book?"

Sighing, Gigi placed her hand over her heart as if wounded. "For shame. That would be breaking rule number three and potentially number six. No screwing those with a connection to your life and no fucking around in the workplace. I left a job over that. I'm not exactly looking to repeat the experience."

Ann was one of the few people who knew about the rules. They'd become fast friends when they met at a mixer for young professionals and discovered they'd been unknowingly sharing the same male companion. Gigi may not engage in relationships but she did abide by strict rules—the first being: all parties must be single. No cheaters were welcome in her bed. Ann was delighted to dodge a bullet and the two women had been friends ever since.

Friendship and trust were two commodities that Gigi didn't deal in often. In life, all you had was your reputation and Gigi guarded hers closely. That's why she had created the rules and cultivated the perfect disguise. She masqueraded as the kind of girl that one would take home to mother, in a package of petite pink innocence, right down to her toe nail polish. The boys liked this virtuous façade too, because despite her rules, she had no trouble filling the space on her proverbial dance card when she wanted it.

"I have your promise then?" Ann's tone had dropped to a level of seriousness normally directed at her employees—not her friends—and with her brow furrowed and lips pressed together, her expression formed a stern mask.

That question—the doubt it implied—made Gigi's eyes burn as the latte soured in her stomach. She looked away. This was the downside of her choices. Logically, Gigi knew that Ann wasn't intentionally slut shaming her. Her friend was protecting someone she cared for. It still made Gigi's skin crawl as though she were nothing more than a cheap whore. She'd promise almost anything to make that feeling go away.

"I promise." Those two small whispered words should have been the easiest she uttered all day. Instead, they etched her throat like acid.

About The Author

CASSIE LEIGH writes contemporary and paranormal romance that is more than skin deep. Before she could write, she began dreaming up stories. Cassie has since moved on from recorded conversations for her dolls on a Fisher-Price cassette player, to novels that draw on her plethora of eccentric passions including Monsters, MMA fighting and Pinup style. Every new obsession seems to find its way into her romance world! She aspires to create character driven drama that have nothing to do with reality. Want more? You can connect with Cassie Leigh online.

https://www.facebook.com/cassieleighauthor
https://www.twitter.com/cassieleigh322
https://www.amazon.com/author/leighcassie

To get the inside track on all new releases, sign up for her newsletter on her web site at
https://www.cassieleighauthor.com

By Cassie Leigh

Haunted Romance Series
Until Death Do Us Part
Follow You Anywhere
Redeem My Broken Soul (coming soon)

Ushers Run Pack
Home For The Howliday

Ink & Brazen Women
Skin Deep
Business Casual
Leading Man (coming soon)
How About Never (coming soon)